THE
GHASTLING

THE Ghastling

BOOK № THREE

Tales of the Macabre, Ghosts and the oh-so Strange

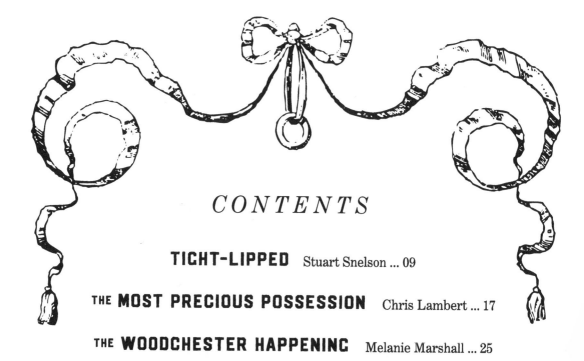

CONTENTS

THE GHASTLING - BOOK THREE

Tales of the Macabre, Ghosts and the oh-so Strange

EDITOR

Rebecca Parfitt

ART DIRECTOR

Nathaniel Winter-Hébert

SOCIAL MEDIA MANAGER

Maria J. Pérez Cuervo

DESIGN BY

Winter-Hébert

winterhebert.com

SPECIAL THANKS TO

Leona Preston

Alyssa Cooper

Catherine Winter-Hébert

CONTACT

Editor@theghastling.com

theghastling.com

facebook.com/theghastling

EDITORIAL

BY

REBECCA PARFITT

THIS IS THE LONG anticipated, eagerly awaited third issue. The tales in this collection hang between the living and the dead. Stories that ask questions about 'mortality' and a surreptitious theme of the 'curse' runs its cloying thread throughout; explores thresholds, interior hauntings and relationships with the inanimate. This time of year sees the release of the 'darker things' we so enjoy reading and watching during winter. The time of year that brings shadows, short days and long nights. So what do we have for you? Well, come closer and I shall tell you.

Calling the Dead explores the unfinished business of the 'recently departed', and is a cautionary tale for the living: do not play with the dead, else they will play with you. In *The Woodchester Happening*, an encounter with a seemingly mute boy leads to a strange and disturbing sequence of events. *A Precious Possession* is a peculiar tale of a box recently inherited, opened, when frankly, it was best left closed... In *The Tower*, a traveller finds himself amongst the ruins of an ancient and foreboding place in rural Eighteenth Century France, beware, reader, of the one who tells the tale... A film crew arrive in rural Spain to observe the rituals of a macabre festival at the site of a drowned village, unaware that they will become a little more than just spectators in *The Village*

Below. *Tight-Lipped* is a chilling tale of what happens when a ventriloquist dies and the grieving are faced with the, now detached, extended entity of the recently deceased. Having lost the extension which gave it life, character, a voice... Sacrilege then surely, to interfere with the ventriloquists' belief to treat the dummy as though it were, in fact, living... *Moth* tells the tale of a young homeless man, recently out of gaol, seeking safety and solitude in a city cemetery but finds himself in unsettling company: the company of a soul collector to be precise...

This collection is not only made to chill the spine but is thought-provoking too. Our ability as humans to believe in the potential of 'otherness' in every living and created thing is one of the best things about being human. To believe that curses fall upon us like an illness and can be passed along by 'carriers'–living or otherwise– makes us wary of the 'something' we don't want to mess with. Our superstition can either plague us or save us... So, once again, dear and precious reader, I advise you to proceed with caution. And if you do find yourself suddenly 'bequeathed', take care.

Enjoy the coming darkness,
Rebecca Parfitt
Editor

TIGHT-LIPPED

BY

STUART SNELSON

THROUGHOUT HIS LIFE, her father had engaged in conversation with his own right hand. These conversations, along with everything else, had now drawn to a close. His lips no longer moved.

Her father's death had left Harry speechless. Should he be buried with her father? She had given this some consideration. To separate them was akin to severing an umbilical connection. How many ventriloquists, she wondered, lay in graves beside their sidekicks? Coffined with his puppet, he would make a curious discovery for future archaeologists; her father's ossified remains beneath those of his perfectly preserved homunculi. In the end, the decision was taken out of her hands. Considering his legacy her father had expressly stated that he wished Harry to survive him.

At the funeral, Harry had been seated, at her father's request, on the altar. Sat mutely beside the coffin, an awkward array of lifeless limbs, he would oversee proceedings. She instantly regretted Harry's presence. Throughout the service, her eyes darted from coffin to puppet and back again. She didn't imagine she was the only one visualising a macabre resurrection, her father, ever the

showman, engaging in switched roles: Harry sitting stoically as frantically her father knocked from inside his coffin, a muffled voice thrown in a perverse reversal of the doll in the suitcase routine. It would be an audacious, if somewhat distressing reappearance. Had a ventriloquist ever performed such an act with either performer or puppet in a coffin? Too dark, perhaps, and certainly not a routine suitable for children's parties. But there would be no curtain call. She had witnessed, first hand, her father's tallowy retreat from life. His coffin lid remained sealed.

As it happened, it was not long before Harry was given voice. He delivered the first of several eulogies, an attempt to invest levity into grave proceedings. Upon the altar, at the priest's intervention, Harry's face flickered onto a television screen, unfocused in close up, the product of shaky, handheld video footage. Disconcertingly detached, his erstwhile manipulator was off camera; Harry's words would only make sense in his master's absence. Through the medium that had served him so well over the course of his career, her father had been allowed this rare, self-eulogising opportunity. It was an irreverent portrait,

SUCH MELANCHOLIC REFLECTION FROM HAND OPERATED MOUTHS MADE FOR A STRANGELY STIRRING SERVICE.

Harry for once, without his master's interruptions, given free reign. Her father's surgically attenuated voice struggled to give life to the doll. Unseen he conjured what he could. The disease's measured onslaught had allowed him time to think, to dwell upon his own mortality, to compose a reflection of his life from his companion's point of view. Considerably weakened, her father could not lend his usual animation to proceedings. Through his tired manipulations, using what strength remained he coaxed the doll into its final performance.

Her father's voice cracking under the gravity of the situation lent Harry a mournful tone; this valediction would be his final vocal appearance. At times one could hear the words catch in his throat, the implication of what he was doing all too clear as he talked of himself in the past tense. This only succeeded in further anthropomorphising this lump of polished wood.

Of the video, she had been unaware. He must have recorded it himself on the ward. At her father's request, she had taken Harry to the hospital, had imagined him giving voice to it late at night, reassuring himself with a palliative rasp. She was initially upset that he hadn't involved her in this epilogue, but soon realised how hard an enterprise it must have been for him. Off screen, unseen, she knew that her father would have been unnecessarily tight-lipped throughout the recording, the consummate professional engaged in a final act of deathbed ventriloquism, showcasing one last time the years of mirrored practice he had endured eradicating his lips' twists.

Hushed, the crowded room had fallen under the Harry's gaze. Sympathies shifted from themselves to this pseudo-orphan, silenced without his partner, his voice taken to the grave. Returned to the world of the inanimate, it was, in a sense, his funeral too. He would remain resolutely mute from now on.

Others followed, offered words of condolence, of celebration, but it was his own summing up, the concise words composed for Harry that would stay with them. His peers, at his request, had brought their other halves. The priest looked out over a congregation of solemn men in black, upon their laps a muted menagerie, the furry and feathered bowed contritely in mourning. More naturally inclined towards mischief and mayhem they were kept in check, availed themselves of the passivity the situation demanded. Taking to the altar, colleagues channelled their grief through their alter egos, persevering valiantly. This was not the stage for quivering lips.

The priest with no small reluctance had complied with the deceased's dying wish. He had been initially uncomfortable with this irreverent interlude, felt that such activity constituted a sacrilegious act. He changed his mind upon seeing first the video eulogy, and then the heartfelt testimonies of his friends. Such melancholic reflection from hand operated mouths made for a strangely stirring service, certainly the most unorthodox he had overseen. He was unaccustomed to such rapt attention, the wide-eyes of a second tier congregation, painted ping-pong ball eyes that seemed fixed upon him. By the end, he had felt oddly bereft without his own puppet. Would that be a way to revitalise his own sermons? He would think it over later, although he suspected that, in the current climate, any activity that could be misconstrued as enticing children was probably best avoided.

Her father visibly bristled when anyone referred to Harry by anything other than his name. Puppet, dummy, doll: all held negative connotations. At the mention, once, of that thing he had halted an interview, indignant, suggested to his questioner that it was rude for her to refer to Harry in such a way whilst he was in the room. Others in his trade favoured the word dummy. Although perfectly descriptive, it felt to him offensive. Puppet suggested more of a marionette, a figure that danced upon strings, and doll he had certainly never cared for. As debates raged, Harry remained resolutely silent on the matter.

Upon diagnosis, her father had been inconsolable. Cancer of the larynx. It seemed such a savage misfortune. His voice had been his life, his career. What cruel punishment was this for a man of his singular talents, severed simultaneously from communication and his work? Thus maligned, he experienced a persecution complex, endured a crisis of faith. He questioned his master's love. Why would his God punish him in this way? Morosely focused, he considered his plight an act of vengeance. What had he done to inspire such rancour? Perhaps his creator had taken offence to his gimcrack golem, his ersatz act of creation, giving life to the inanimate, voicing the silent. Alone, in hospital, he punished himself; passed slow time engaged in morbid self-assessment, trawled his life for evidence of wrongdoing. What could he have done to warrant such treatment?

Awaiting his laryngectomy he took solace from time spent with his fellow ventriloquists. Perhaps only they could fully sympathise with his predicament, the unusual symbiotic situation of not just losing one's own voice but that of one's companion. In private, they each breathed a sigh of relief, offered silent prayers to the effect that they would not become similarly afflicted.

Although the operation had been considered a success, her father died shortly after. Complications were cited, but she felt, in her heart, that he had conceded defeat. With his doctor, he had talked through options regarding the restoration of his voice, but he knew that it would never be the same. He was reluctant to adjust to a reconstructed future.

Dolefully, she contemplated never hearing Harry's voice again, their conversations over. She decided to put him away for the wake, his presence, she imagined, would only be distressing. She was wary also of some drunken transgression, of the possibility that some inebriated mourner would fumble him into position on their laps and try to give voice to him. Whilst she was sure such trespass would go against some unvoiced code of honour, would be akin to touching up a colleague's wife, she thought it best to remove temptation. Even the thought of such an action filled her with dread, an impostor's infringement, the puppet's movements mirroring their own inebriated states. She would not bear witness to such manhandling.

As friends of her father's – fellow ventriloquists, variety circuit stalwarts – made their way back to her house she knew that she would be uncomfortable now in Harry's silenced presence, of what his silence would constantly remind her. At her house, it seemed less a wake and more a lugubrious children's party. Her father had requested that events proceed more in celebration than lamentation. But the manner in which one's funeral unfolded was rarely the domain of the deceased. Sombre ventriloquists contemplated not only their own mortality but also that of their puppets. What had always hovered as a negative inevitability they had now seen so starkly illustrated. Guzzling gottles of geer, puppets on one hand, drinks in the other, they drowned dual sorrows.

On her sofa, seated, a line of attendant puppets; their manipulators, giving their arms a break, continued discussions of their future without them present. They imparted a chilling stillness, a disconcerting tranquillity. In the garden, without their charges, her father's friends were reduced to a humble humdrum, their mischievous sides apparently only emerging in the presence of their puppets. Silenced were the bad tempered arguments they constructed, engaged in wholeheartedly, the embodiments of split personalities.

They speculated sombrely upon the future of their craft. Her own thoughts, which under the circumstances she decided to keep to herself, were far from optimistic. She imagined that in the future ventriloquism would take some explaining, a pursuit anachronistic in the twentieth century, never mind the twenty-first. In their words, she heard echoes of her father's. Throughout her life, he had talked of the death of the variety circuit – a whole host of acts who no longer had a place to perform, no natural habitat. By the end, he entertained the lesser echelons: children's parties, the occasional cruise. The range of suitable environments in which they could perform had narrowed distinctly. They were considered end-of-the-pier entertainers; from pantomime posters they would reluctantly beam.

Her father had witnessed his peers try to keep abreast of the times, to arrest ventriloquisms slip into quaint archaism. As careers faded, he had noted a glut of vulgar puppets, sexual lasciviousness sitting oddly upon furry lips. Their doll's cheek progressed from inopportune interference to full-scale salacity, crossing from children's to adult entertainment by aide of profanity, a tirade of expletives to engage late-night drunken audiences. It seemed a cheap upheaval. Over the years, Harry's personality had developed almost autonomously. He would not throw that away to draw tawdry laughs from pie-eyed throngs. To the end, he had stuck to his principles.

Visiting her father for the last time in the chapel of rest, she had taken Harry along, had allowed him to gaze down upon his stricken master. She half anticipated a thrown voice, for him once more to impose his personality. His cold lips clamped rigidly together, there would be no shattering of the deathly silence. She experienced a confusion of emotions, felt almost as though Harry, to a degree, was undergoing a more rigorous bereavement than she herself was. Whilst fully aware that she was projecting, in her hands Harry couldn't help but look forlorn, lifeless. Without her father to provide voice, to provide movement, he looked a shell of himself. Such was testament to her father's abilities, the life that he had engendered. Both silent now, she felt odd standing between them. Where once their union guaranteed chaos, now there was simply calm. She resisted the urge to lay him alongside her father, to draw her fingers downwards over the puppet's eyelids and leave him nestled upon her father's arm. Feeling ridiculous, but obliged nonetheless, she lowered Harry's wooden lips to her father's lest he may kiss him goodbye.

She had grown up in Harry's presence; he had been there since she was born. She made no false claims to remember him as a toddler, but there were certainly photographs aplenty to testify to their interactions, a Polaroid camera put through its paces capturing their initial intimacy. Looking back

SHE ENGAGED IN LATE NIGHT CONFESSIONALS DURING WHICH SHE WHISPERED INTO HIS CHIPPED, VARNISHED EAR, HER DARKEST SECRETS.

now, she considered her actions as a child, their changing relationship. She had shifted from unconditional love to sibling rivalry. She realised, of course, that to be jealous of the inanimate was a ludicrous position. Nevertheless, she had experienced moments of extraordinary envy. Witnessing his treatment at her parents' hands, the attention lavished upon him, his mollycoddled existence, she sensed that they considered him their favourite. After all, he only answered back when he was made to. During darker periods she had hatched revenge, had imagined enacting all manner of grisly dismemberment upon his vulnerable body, limbs trimmed under cover of sawdust. But try as she might she could never hurt him.

Growing up with him had proved a mixed blessing. Visitors were often surprised that he didn't sit with them in the living room, although her father never required much encouragement before Harry made an appearance. But what was amusing as a child became an embarrassment as an adolescent, at least publicly. Her father was quick to sense this shift, became a more tempered presence when her friends visited.

Never aging, over time Harry went from being an older brother to a younger one. This had been a strange cognitive experience. Her eventual realisation that one day he would be silenced, led to considerations of her own mortality. It was a subject upon which she had been reluctant to dwell. She was forced to dwell upon it now.

In an odd sense, she had never felt like an only child; her wooden brother had certainly filled a gap. It stood in tribute to her father's gift that he felt, at times, like an independent presence, albeit one who didn't have much to say when left to his own devices. Now she experienced a double bereavement, losing both her father and proxy sibling simultaneously. Anxious through her teenage years he became

repository for her secrets. She engaged in late night confessionals during which she whispered into his chipped, varnished ear, her darkest secrets. She would be thrilled seeing Harry on television with her father knowing that he had heard all her secrets but would never be able to disclose them. To whom did other girls tell their secrets?

It had been a family enterprise. Whilst her father gave Harry life, offstage it was her mother who bathed him, washed him down and ensured he looked his best. It was her mother who laboured, behind the scenes, handstitching a plethora of costumes for him, it being difficult to buy off the peg for puppets. Appearing on television, he was always resplendent in some new handmade creation. In the house, he even had his own wardrobe, a rack of arrested fashions. That he seemed to have more clothes than she did was yet another source of envy.

Following her mother's death, her father had stretched his repertoire from two to three as he endeavoured to fill several roles simultaneously. Again, during this time she had taken an odd solace from the doll's presence, a sense, at least, of continuity.

She kept her father's last words in a box. After the operation he could no longer speak, was reduced to the written word. She found consolation in these scribbled fragments following his death, this box of one-sided conversations, final thoughts frozen in time. Often despondent she would pull randomly, scraps from the box and in his voice hear words never spoken, his voice thrown from beyond the grave.

It took her some time before she could sit down and watch videos of them recorded from television. She felt privileged that she had a visual record of them in their prime, how many bereaved relatives could make such claims? She was keen to oversee an archive, that her father's career, in as ephemeral an art as it was, would be at the very least, catalogued. Eventually she would make her way through the boxes of related paraphernalia.

She was uncertain what she would do with him now. She had heard about a place in America, a museum for ventriloquist's dolls. Although she had never been, it struck her as quite a melancholy notion. Room upon room of muted puppets, the formerly mischievous now sedate, their inopportune wisecracks forever silenced, cheeky smirks arrested. Could she really consign Harry to such a fate?

From a cupboard, she emptied a cast of also-rans. Her father had tried to expand his act, broaden his ventriloquial family, but with limited success. They had failed to take hold. Neither his verbally dexterous renderings nor his skilled manipulations could inject them with life, something was always absent from them. The public's reception proved as lukewarm as her own. He conceded that he would only fully inhabit one doll. Regarding them now, this raft of animals, wooden and plastic pretenders, she sighed. At least their disposal would find no obstacle.

If she kept Harry, what role would he play in her life? Was it too late to reinstate him as her confidant, for him to be once more the recipient of her secrets? Not that she possessed any secrets or scandals that needed to be shared. If she resumed her conversations with him, her most shameful confession would be that she engaged in conversation with a puppet. She would focus instead on her flesh and blood relationships, conversations that consisted of more than one voice.

In anticipation of future relationships, she did not relish the prospect of explaining Harry's significance. How did she live around him without repelling suitors? There's someone I would like you to meet, she imagined explaining before his rickety limbs were unfolded from a suitcase. She had problems making relationships work as it was; she required no outside help in dissuading potential partners. When would be the right time to introduce him?

She put off administering the estate for as long as possible. She knew that her father had been reluctant to address her mother's material aftermath, that with her father's death she had inherited that task as well. What did she dread discovering? A puppet of her mother, fashioned after her death to keep him company? Did he ever get lonely? She found it hard to imagine a ventriloquist as ever being truly alone. She realised that what she faced were not normal considerations for the bereaved. To some degree their novelty helped take her mind off her own grief.

It was some weeks after the funeral, before she finally steeled herself to the task of going through her parent's possessions.

She discovered the photograph beneath the lining of her mother's jewellery box, its edges thinned by fingerprints. In the photograph, her mother held within her arms a newborn baby. But something wasn't right, something was slightly skew. The expression on her mother's face was one of restrained sombreness, the ghosts of tears upon her face. She focused on the baby's face. Its eyes closed, its limbs too stiff, it was no longer of this world. Who was it, this inanimate wrinkle of a thing?

As she held the photograph, this diminished image, she imagined her mother cradling it, a life evaporated. A nurse on the ward had offered to take a photograph by way of morbid memorial, had ushered into the frame the most emotionally wrought picture she would take. Had they known long before delivery what awaited them?

Paperclipped to the photograph: a medical certificate, a registration of stillbirth. Her brother. It felt odd even thinking in such terms. She took in the date. He had been three years her senior. Reading the certificate, she silently mouthed his name, a name that had been on her lips all her life without realising its significance.

She regretted, now, her father's failure to go through her mother's effects. Had he known of her melancholy memento? Her mind flooded with questions. Would there have been a burial? She was unfamiliar with the protocol surrounding stillbirths. Perhaps they were dealt with on site at the hospital, a euphemism concealing its disposal, a prayer before incineration.

From her own limited experience, she knew that people dealt with such tragedies differently. Some opted to celebrate the deceased's birthday, to give life, of a sort, to their loved one, incidentally prolonging their own suffering. Her parents had evidently chosen a more secretive policy. She felt a sense of betrayal that they had kept this to themselves all these years, had chosen not to talk about it, yet in a warped way memorialised him every day of their lives. Was her father's talent born of sadness?

She was amazed that they had maintained their secret. Inevitably, she reassessed her past, trawled for substantiating evidence, of anniversaries starkly marked. It was testament to them, to their well-intentioned façade, that she could recall nothing. Would there have been any benefit in telling her? Had her birth freed them from his shadow. Without her would they have survived together or would they have stumbled on, lost, grieving, in perpetual reminisce until eventually breaking down?

What function had Harry fulfilled for her father? Stand-in, replacement, continuation? To what extent had her father's conversations with Harry become cathartic? A beloved puppet used as a coping mechanism. Her questions would fail to find answers. No relatives survived who could throw light upon her discovery; answers had been taken to the grave. That he had handled his sadness in this manner just made her miss him more, had attempted god like acts in order to have the son they seemed doomed not to have. She felt bad that he had never fully given voice to his sorrows.

She wondered whether they had intended to tell her at some point. After years of non disclosure when would have been the right time? Maybe they worried that such a revelation would cast too dark a shadow over her father's practise. She found it frustrating that there was no one left with whom to express her sadness, to question about events.

For one who made his voice his career, her father could be surprisingly taciturn, a garrulousness that abandoned him when he set the doll down. During her childhood as she whispered her darkest thoughts into Harry's ear, were others engaged in such activity? Had he served a similar function for her father, become a repository of his crises? Her mother too, perhaps, had bent his ear. She suspected, as she gazed at Harry, that he held all the answers, had been privy to everything she now wished to know. They were secrets he would not be sharing.

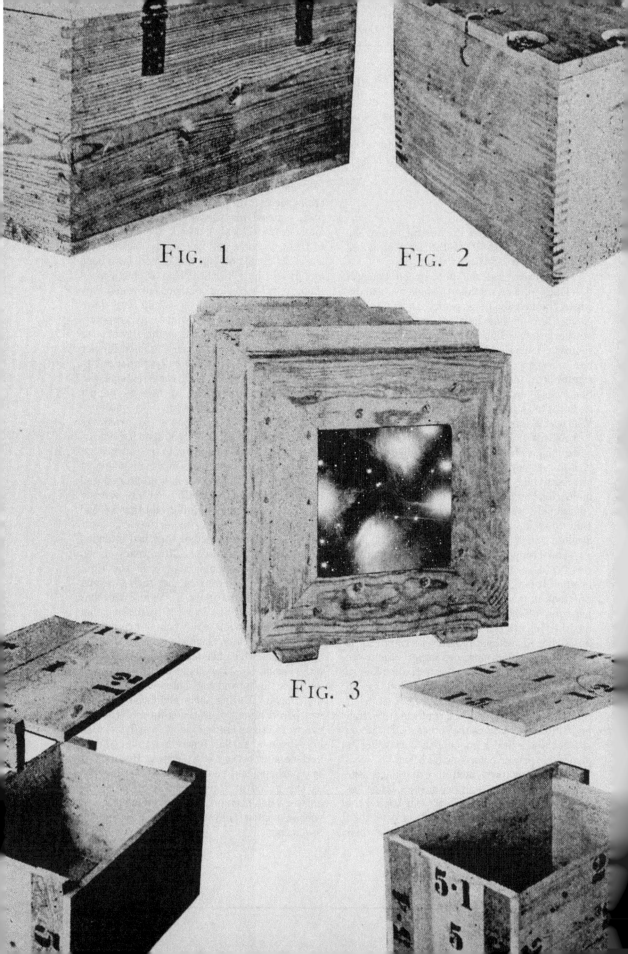

FIG. 1

FIG. 2

FIG. 3

THE
MOST PRECIOUS POSSESSION
BY
CHRIS LAMBERT

A MONTH AFTER his great uncle passed away, Robert found himself sitting in a dark wood-panelled office listening to the dry rusted tock of an unseen and ancient time-piece. Uncle Peter had been a curious soul. Robert's mother, who had passed away three years previously, had described her younger brother as 'unknowable'. They had not been close as children. She had been sent to a third rate boarding school for emotionally detached girls, whilst he, inexplicably, had been home-schooled. When they had been reunited during the summer holidays, he mainly kept to his room, only venturing out to eat or to make his toilet. On occasions, sitting at either end of the vast dining room table, she would try to engage him in polite conversation. She would enquire as to how he was spending his time and he would expound at length on the maps he had studied or the ancient tomes he had researched. He would repeat long passages of ancient text in Anglo-Saxon, Nordic, Ancient Greek, Latin or in other lost languages she could not fathom. For a child of eleven years old his prodigious knowledge was deeply disquieting.

Robert's mother and Peter were both wards of a kindly priest; The Reverend Stanthorpe. Their parents had died within a few months of each other. The kindly Stanthorpe and his wife ensured that their final wishes were carried out.

An impressive private fortune was sensibly divided to pay for the children's schooling, books and future welfare, as a well as a handsome sum to cover the Stanthorpe's needs.

It was Peter's vociferous obsession with books that always struck his sister as strange and somewhat suspect. Why was he not scrambling up trees, muddying his nose or fighting with the other urchins who lived on the street at the end of the drive?

The Reverend Stanthorpe often commented on how alike Peter was to his late father. Both were very private souls, obsessed with the written word and prone to fits of prolonged daydreaming. The Reverend would go so far as to describe these episodes as fugue states. Peter was no stranger to these. On several occasions, when eating one of Mrs Stanthorpe's delicious suppers, his sister caught him staring straight ahead, a forked potato floating an inch from his mouth, his eyes glazed. She shifted from left to right, and, seeing that her movement caused no reaction, she waved her hand before his face. He would sit like this until his food went cold. Nothing would stir him. Not a waving hand, a sudden clap or a glass of water in the face. Peter's father was much the same. The Reverend Stanthorpe had known him since childhood. He had seen his eyes grow blank in his sermons, which struck him as strange as he prided himself on scintillating and exciting talks of sin and hellfire. He remembered once taking tea with him. As he was sipping at a cup of Darjeeling, the saucer fell from his hands, the cup smashed to pieces on the floor and his mouth hung open. From his open mouth there seemed to escape a strangely familiar tune. He sat for a few minutes before blinking and continuing the conversation as though nothing had happened. The Reverend was surprised and concerned. He explained what he had witnessed.

"So sorry," Peter's father had laughed. "I stepped out for a moment."
They never spoke of it again.

Uncle Peter had been much the same in his adult years. Robert recalled, as he sat listening to the slow ticking of the ancient clock, of several such absences he himself had witnessed. On one occasion he had discovered Uncle Peter sitting at his desk, frozen, pen in hand, ink pooling from the nib. After several minutes Uncle Peter had stirred, continuing to write, ignoring the smudge of deep blue marking the page.

The rusted mechanism inside the old clock creaked on. Robert checked his pocket watch against the decrepit timepiece. Had he really been sitting here for over an hour? It seemed so. He rose from the chair, examining the room again. Dusty books of law and faded framed certificates adorned the shelves and walls. Yellow edged receipts, skewered on a dirty upright spike, sat on the battered desk. Finally a footfall outside. Robert returned to his seat. The door groaned open. Mr Talchester stepped inside. His back was hunched, sweat dripping down his wrinkled pink face. His wiry white hair seemed caught mid-dance, each strand attempting a different step, out of time with the others. He wheezed. In his hands he held a small wooden box.

"So sorry to keep you," he mumbled, shuffling over to the other side of his tired oak desk. "There were so many locks, boxes within boxes, the final combination had seventeen digits."
Robert gave a supportive smile. Mr Talchester fluttered over to the desk.
"Your Uncle Peter insisted, you see. Insisted."
Robert smiled again.
"Once all the affairs were in order, you see." Mr Talchester paused and looked at Robert with concern. "I trust you are happy with the house?"
"It was most generous of Uncle Peter to leave

ROBERT LOOKED AT THE WOODEN BOX IN THE SOLICITOR'S HANDS. "WHAT IS IT?"

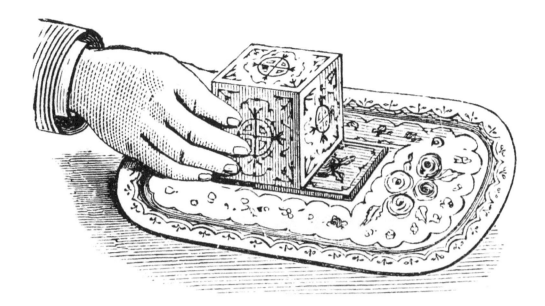

it to me," Robert said.

"There was no-one else. We checked thoroughly."

"Still. We had very little to do with one another."

"He was a very private man."

"Indeed."

Mr Talchester cleared his throat. "As I said, once all the other affairs were in order, he said that you must have this."

Robert looked at the wooden box in the solicitor's hands. "What is it?"

Mr Talchester looked down. "I do not have a single idea. He said it was his most precious possession."

Robert held out his hand.

Mr Talchester paused, unmoving. "I must confess to being very curious."

"That is most natural."

"I also must confess that I was most tempted to look inside."

"Did you?"

"I am sorry to say that I attempted to do so, but I could not open it."

Robert smiled. "Well, my uncle was a quiet eccentric. Knowing him it is probably nothing more than a trinket, an old piece of bark or a pigeon feather."

Mr Talchester walked forward and placed the box in Robert's outstretched hands.

The box was made of a plain light brown beech. Its surface was scratched and in some places gouged. The lid was hinged but there appeared to be no discernible lock or catch.

"Can you hear that?"

Mr Talchester had stood suddenly, his head cocked to one side, a finger to his lips. Robert frowned, all he could hear was the clock. Mr Talchester strode over to the timepiece, opened the little door below the rusting face, stopping the pendulum with his fingertips.

"Listen."

Robert listened. A small tinkle of music could be heard. A slow familiar tune. A waltz? As he listened the music seemed to grow in volume. As it grew there was the tiniest of clicks. The black line between lid and box thickened, growing larger. The music began to soar. The lid floated open. Mr Talchester leaned over to look. Robert peered inside.

"Sir," he said, waving his hand. "You are blocking the light."

Mr Talchester mumbled an apology, stepping back. This did not seem to remedy the problem, for the inside of the box was the deepest and darkest black Robert had ever seen.

The music soared, reaching a crescendo, it was as though more music boxes were joining the fray. The tinkle of comb against pin becoming unbearably loud.

Robert stood, carrying the open box to the lamp on the desk. He placed it under the glow of the bulb. The inside was black.

"Incredible," Mr Talchester gasped. "It must be made of jet or some other dark stone."

Robert did not speak, the music started to slow. The teeth of the comb biting the pins of the

Fig. 3

drum at longer intervals. Robert let his fingers explore the inside of the box. He drew his hand back suddenly. Mr Talchester leaned forward.

"What is it?"

Robert put the box down. He ran his finger around the rim.

"The rim is there, but the inside is not."

"I beg your pardon?"

"The box has no inside."

Mr Talchester's eyes widened. "Again, I beg your pardon."

"I cannot find the sides. This is most unusual."

Robert held his hand above the open box. Taking a deep breath he clenched his fist and lowered it inside. The box, which appeared from the outside to be little deeper than an average sized teapot, covered his hand to the wrist. Robert let his hand drop further.

"It has no bottom," he cried, as he sank his arm to the elbow. Soon the box covered his thin upper arm stopping at shoulder. Mr Talchester gripped the desk for support.

"This is not of God," he spoke, crossing himself.

Robert pulled his arm from the box. He stood up straight, eyeing the box with fear and curiosity.

The tune ground to a stop.

"Thank heavens," gasped Mr Talchester, mopping his brow. Robert stepped forward, slamming the lid shut.

"Well," he said. "Uncle Peter was certainly an eccentric."

"He was more than that, sir. What has he bequeathed you?"

"Did it come with a message for me? Some instructions?"

"Nothing, sir."

"I do not wish to open it again."

"I trust you will not."

"And yet, it is rather fascinating, do you not think?"

"Perhaps your uncle has a book on the matter in his library."

Robert laughed. "Have you seen his library? Where would I even begin?"

Mr Talchester walked to the door. He pulled it open most violently and leant against it.

"I am a simple man sir. And I have seen something this afternoon that I should like to forget. I would appreciate it, sir, if you would take your uncle's most strange possession from here at once. The thought of it is making me quite giddy."

Robert nodded. Picking up the box, he walked to the door, extending his hand for Mr Talchester to shake. Mr Talchester turned away.

"Your hand, sir," he shuddered. "I do not trust where it has been."

Robert nodded again. He turned on his heel and left the solicitor's office, flinching slightly as the door slammed heavily behind him.

Later that same day, Robert stood staring at the box on his desk. He could hear the music from within.

"But I have not wound it," he thought. "For there is nothing to wind."

The music played on. Robert pulled down the lid on his desk, locking his study door before drifting to bed.

Robert did not sleep. He lay in the dark watching the moonlight play on the ceiling. He could feel the box in the room below. Feel the click of tooth on pin. Feel the cool space inside. His hand waving in the dark air. He could feel the nothing. Feel the cold black vacuum. He started to hum. A strangely familiar tune. A sweet sound. His tongue clicked on the spoke of his teeth in time with the tune from below.

Robert sat up. He stopped the hum but could feel it welling up inside. Could hear it within his skull, within his throat, his gullet, his stomach, his heart. Leaping out of bed he threw himself to the floor. He pressed his ear to the rug. There it was! The singing box, muffled but distinct. He pulled back the rug to listen again. Ear on wood. There. Louder now. So sweet. So delicious.

His hum became a song now. A song, sweet and sour, bitter and salt on his tongue.

He stood. His voice soared. Roared out into the night. The music was so loud now. He could feel it deep in the hidden gore of his bones.
"Sing with me," chanted the teeth of the comb.
"Dance with me," called the pins on the drum.

Robert danced his answer through the door and down the stairs. He danced his answer turning the lock, pushing the door and entering the room. He danced his answer at the roll top desk, watching it rise to reveal the beautiful scratched and gouged beech box beneath.

The lid was open.

Robert and the box sang together. His eyes glazed, his mouth moving. The music slowed. Robert kept in time. Slower and slower. Teeth hit pin for a final time. The lid swung shut.

Robert stared at the box in silence. He stood utterly still in the near dark. He stayed that way until morning. His face frozen in a satisfied smile.

Mr Talchester opened the door reluctantly on the third knock. Robert stood in the porch.
"What is it?" the old solicitor's voice quavered.
"I am sorry to bother you at this hour."
"It is noon."
Robert grinned. "I hope I have not interrupted an early luncheon."
"You have not."
"May I come in?"
Mr Talchester bit his lip. "Do you have it with you?"
"Do I have what?"
"The music box."
Robert shook his head with a vague smile. "Oh that," he said. "It is safely stowed away."
Mr Talchester sighed, stepped to one side, allowing Robert to walk into the hall.
"Will you be staying long?" Mr Talchester asked, trying not to show his discomfort, but failing.
Robert raised an eyebrow with a hint of indignation. "I have only just arrived, sir."
Mr Talchester grimaced. "I apologise, sir. It is just that your last visit played havoc with my

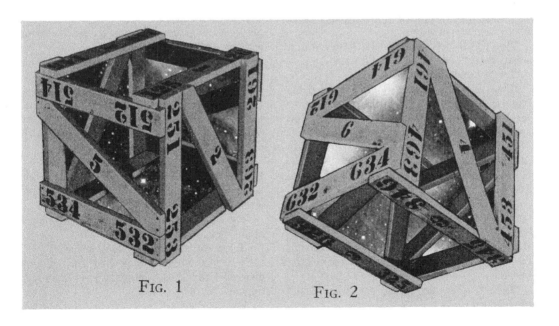

FIG. 1   FIG. 2

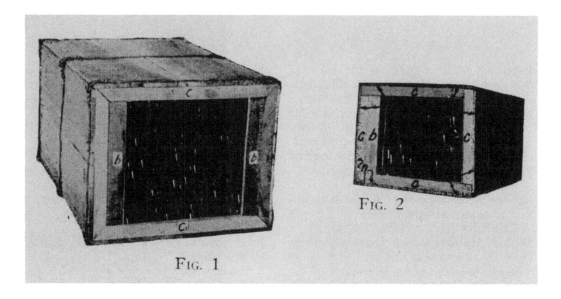

FIG. 1

FIG. 2

nerves."

Robert nodded. "I understand."

"Would you care for some tea?"

"I would be much obliged."

Mr Talchester rang a bell. After speaking to his maid they made their way to the study. Robert sat in silence as the maid poured the tea. As she left, Mr Talchester spoke.

"What brings you here?" he asked.

Robert waited for the door to shut, for the handle to turn before he gave his reply.

"I have some unfinished business with you regarding the possession my uncle passed on to me."

"I see. Did you need to see the paperwork? Everything was in order."

"Was it?" Robert fixed Mr Talchester with a steady gaze. "I am not sure that it was."

"I do not understand."

"Then I shall explain." Robert steepled his fingers. "You can read, Mr Talchester?"

Mr Talchester's eyes widened. "Although you are my client, I am disturbed by your tone."

"I would like to trust that my late uncle's solicitor can read."

Mr Talchester harrumphed. "I can. Why do you ask?"

"Perhaps you could take a look at the instructions Uncle Peter gave you regarding the music box."

Hands shaking, Mr Talchester leafed through the papers on his desk. He pulled out a grey folder.

"Turn to the third page, paragraph four," commanded Robert.

Mr Talchester found the section with his trembling finger.

Robert stood slowly. "What does it say?"

Mr Talchester cleared his throat. His voice all a quiver. "The client instructs that only the recipient of the item must be present when it is examined."

"You can read," Robert smiled. "Good. I am assuming you read this instruction before you brought me the box?"

"I did," said Mr Talchester, his eyes narrowing. "But, may I ask, when did you have the opportunity to read these words yourself?"

"I never read them, Mr Talchester."

"Then how…"

"I wrote them."

Mr Talchester sprang to his feet. "You are toying with me, sir!"

"I assure you, Mr Talchester, that I am doing nothing of the sort."

"Your Uncle Peter wrote them. Years ago. When you were a child."

"He did not. I did."

Mr Talchester shook his head. "This is madness," he mumbled.

Robert laughed. It was a bored laugh. An old laugh. A laugh that had been here before and would be here again.

"The consequences for your transgression are quite fascinating."

Mr Talchester spluttered, "Consequences?"

"Yes, you did not think that such blatant disregard for Uncle Peter's wishes would go unpunished, did you?"

"I was curious."

"YOUR HAND, SIR," HE SHUDDERED. "I DO NOT TRUST WHERE IT HAS BEEN."

"Well, I can assure you that your curiosity will be satisfied."

Mr Talchester moved to the door.

"I – I think you should leave," he stammered. Robert laughed again. It sounded hollow, false and strangely distant. He sank back into his chair.

"I shall leave for a moment," he said with a smile. "I won't be long."

The smile was frozen to his face, but he did not move from his seat. As Mr Talchester watched, Robert's body relaxed, his shoulders slumped and his head fell forward. Mr Talchester remained by the door. He was determined not to move. Robert stared at the floor. His jaw slowly sagged. Mr Talchester stood stock still, staring at the prone form of his former client. Several moments passed. The dry old tock of the clock echoed around the silent study. Robert's body was utterly still. Mr Talchester could not see if he was breathing.

"Damn the man," he thought. "I have no love for the fellow, but if he has died I will have a deuce of a time explaining it."

Mr Talchester edged away from the door. Robert did not respond to the creak of the floorboards. He did not stir as the elderly solicitor crept ever closer. In the distance Mr Talchester thought he could hear the faint sound of a music box. The old familiar tune. The teeth picking at the pins of the comb inside. Mr Talchester shook his head. Robert had certainly not brought the box with him. The old solicitor reached out a hand, pushing at Robert's right shoulder. Robert rocked back, his head lolled, hanging at an obscene angle. The tune was slightly louder now. Mr Talchester leant forward, he could not tell, even this close, if his visitor was breathing. As he leant even closer, hoping to feel a light exhalation on his cheek, he suddenly leapt back with a start. The old familiar tune was coming from deep within Robert's gaping maw. Louder and louder it rang out; teeth against comb, teeth against comb, teeth against comb. Spiralling out from the dark of his gullet, over the tongue and past the parted teeth.

Mr Talchester backed away to the door. He kept his eyes fixed on the horror before him. His hand tried to find the handle. As his fingers closed over the sweet comfort of the metal, the music ceased. Robert's head slowly raised. He sat up in the chair. He carefully closed his gaping mouth and smiled.

"So sorry," he said. "I stepped out for a moment."

Mr Talchester could not speak. He turned the handle. Robert rose from his chair.

"Where are you going, Mr Talchester?"

The door swung open. Mr Talchester gasped in relief, his eyes locked on Robert's. He could not see the dark void gaping behind him. The corridor gone.

"I said that your curiosity would be satisfied, sir."

Mr Talchester turned his head. He saw the darkness beyond and let out a muffled cry. The old familiar tune echoed loudly from the Stygian blackness. Mr Talchester gibbered and moaned. He turned back to the room, frozen in disbelief. Robert stepped forward and put a hand upon Mr Talchester's chest. He pushed. Mr Talchester tripped and stumbled back through the doorway. Spiralling through the black towards the magnified sound of teeth and comb.

Robert reached for the handle and pulled the door shut. The music stopped.

There was a knock. Upon opening the door, Robert was unsurprised to see the maid standing with an empty tray in her hand.

"I've come to clear the things," she said. She looked about the room. "Where is the master?" Robert smiled, "He had to step out for a while. He did not say when he would be back. Now, if you'll excuse me, I must get back to my books."

Robert smiled at the maid, strode down the corridor, out through the front door and into the early afternoon, whistling an old and familiar tune.

T H E

WOODCHESTER HAPPENING

BY

MELANIE MARSHALL

THE TEAM of volunteers and I descended upon Woodchester Park at lunchtime yesterday. I stayed in the car park tying my walking boots extra tight and heaving bottles of water from the Land Rover. By the time I'd done, I just caught sight of Josie's red scarf disappearing behind her down the track. I did one last check to make sure they hadn't forgotten anything: tuneable detectors, sunset timetable, compass, OS map, boxes, torches and metal tags; then locked up, knowing I wouldn't catch the rest of them until we reached the pit of the valley.

I set off: sun on my skin, iPod in ears, The Cure my soundtrack to coasting wood pigeons and breaths of dung-filled air. The walk would me good, according to Dr Hall; my weekends are so often spent crouched in caves and church towers like some sort of hunchback that I welcomed the stretch in my muscles and the soil and foliage sticking to my trousers, slithers of copper on corduroy. Just as the path hollowed out from under me, so the umbrella of branches thickened above that I could hardly see the sky. My arms strained under the weight of the rucksack and bottles and I faltered, cursing that cancelled gym membership for a subscription to the Ecologist. From the undergrowth, in an instant, a little lad ran out in front of me, wearing shorts, his knees bowed like

a leveret's. I stopped dead.

"Alright mate," I called, cautious to stay out of his path. You can't be too careful these days.

He nodded, shaking pudding-basin hair.

"Where's your mum or dad?"

No reaction. Twigs and filigree leaves sieved the beams of sun. His head was ablaze in the light. I wondered then what I'd do if he suddenly began to cry or scream.

"You'd better go and find whoever you're here with." I tried to sound stern.

He looked at me. Something crunched in the bracken. Far off, the cackling of a pheasant, or maybe a partridge. The boy raised an arm and pointed the way back to where I'd come from. I looked behind me to unflinching sycamores and ferns, nothing untoward. But he just stood there pointing and pointing, mouth agape and eyes glossy. In the end I left him to it. Odd child.

Elderberries suspended in huge bunches like bulging testes, blackberries were dusted in chalk. The deer park, void of its intended inhabitants, was full of cows, white-topped black – velvet pints of stout. Some of that bitterness would do me now. Out here, away from the cars and pubs, your mood can change so quickly. You wake up on the sunniest of days and suddenly everything's dark. With the chill firmly in my bones, I reached

THE HOUSE WAS LEFT LIKE THIS, UNFINISHED, TOOLS DOWNED AND BOOTS ABANDONED IN 1874

the mansion site at gone three thirty. The house sits in a bowl of green in which not a train or jet engine can be heard. Its masonry is sufficiently crumbled to be called a ruin, although there are floors and windows in the east wing. It's a Victorian Gothic revival, so I've read. Old Alan sat underneath the buttress wrapping his mouth around a crustless cheese sarnie – he's a revival too. Someone dug him up from somewhere.

"Ewen's here," he said to the rest.

A few of them shuffled around their tripods and detectors, muttering. Carl's whinnying echoed round the site, he had Josie in a piggyback and her thighs properly clenched him. Slag. The large lead tongues of four stone animals protrude from corners of the roof – two wolves, a boar, an eagle. The clock is being restored by a horologist and is generally not wound. The house was left like this, unfinished, tools downed and boots abandoned in 1874. Historians don't agree on why. Stones loosened, weather festered at its core for over a century, so a gargoyle launching itself from the ledge and pulverizing Carl's skull wouldn't have gone amiss.

I gathered the team together to dish out jobs, despite their complaints.

"We've got work to do," I said.

The two new women grimaced and whispered something to one another. They'd pitched their tents to the south of the building in view of the first of five lakes that lined the valley. Josie's, decorated with bright daisies, was nearest the woods. My tent was still in the bag. Nevermind, I got my favourite task – grabbing the brush and jam jar I yelled, "Gonna get me some guano."

No one replied. Bat crap to them. The sun was due to set at 18.27; at 18.31 a gleam still cut through the clouds. I scaled the spiral staircase of the South tower, deep into pale stone – umber in places, dove grey and ivory. Further I went into moss-smell, reflections in the leaded casements like dirty puddles. Except for a beam from which the bell would have swung, the tower was a

quivering fur colonies. Fascinating creatures and far better company than Homo sapiens. Less audible, they purr and click when they mate, gorge on gnats and shit pure gold. In the few weeks we've been coming here, scouting out the area, I've learnt a lot, and not just about bats. The others had careers, families, sex lives. I borrowed books and visited websites about the nineteenth-century owner, Lord William Leigh, and his daughters Blanche and Beatrice, right little Ophelias by all accounts. Before, Roman occupation, and centuries after, a WWII billet for Canadian troops. So many dawns and twilights since, and my capacity for knowledge was infinite.

At dusk, three pipistrelle emerged from apertures in the stonework. Urged their little bodies out and trickled into the blue. They flitted over the ice house, stalked insects on the surface of the lakes, chattering in an ultrasound even the heterodyne machine couldn't detect. I whispered their ancient name as they flew away: 'Vesper', hoping they'd hear me. From up there, Josie looked even further away. She was helping the others, stopping to ask about their children or whether they wanted tea from the flask. I could make out her smile, or perhaps she was yawning. Turning to the woods, the vertigo I normally enjoy took me over. Iron air coated my lungs and I went dizzy. Voices, footsteps on the stairs, figures in the trees – all the history of the place was bearing down on me. I steadied myself on the ledge. In the woods, in my mind, the strange boy still lurked.

I returned, recovered from my episode, with a jar of shit. By 21.45 I'd pitched the tent in the dark. They'd constructed a bonfire without me and were singing, drinking Captain Morgan. Old Alan winked and offered me a sup, sticky rum and tin mug against my teeth. Josie, mouth masked by red scarf, was supposed to be manning the sonar equipment, but I didn't have the heart to tell her off.

"How's the job?" she said, cheeks glowing

across the fire.

Not now, don't ask me that now, I thought. "I lost it."

Carl was on my side of the circle. Josie's eyes flicked over and she tried not to laugh.

"I thought you loved Pet Superstore. I thought animal welfare was your thing."

Lesser and greater horseshoes and long-eared bats are my thing. You are my thing. I can hardly recall why they sacked me. Something about discourtesy to a customer. A dead dog. I don't remember. Days gather together now like clouds of midges and I can't be bothered with memories. It didn't matter; the volunteers were off their faces by midnight. Through the smoke, old women gargled rum, Alan nodded off, Carl unzipped his fleece for Josie and wrapped her up like a prize. Not sure what time I turned in, my Seiko was on the blink and there was only one bar on my phone. The intention was for us to rise again just before dawn, the prime hunting hour of bats.

In dreams or half-slumber, I awoke to the distinct toll of a bell, very loud, very clear. No other sounds. Obscured by a porridgy light, gradually my eyes became accustomed. I sat up and brushed my head on the canvas, wetting my hair. I clambered out of the tent, saw the embers of the bonfire and smelt a smoky frost. Cows began lowing in the park, their moos growing louder and louder as if they were being prodded. Shivering, I realised I was the only human awake, and no bats fluttered in the moonshine. Trying to focus on what was ahead of me, I lumbered over to the mansion's front wall. Another toll rang out

across the valley. Where the hell was it coming from? Rational thoughts flew from me. The cows' distress amplified. I don't know why I looked up; perhaps I expected to see a pipistrelle, but as I did, a face appeared at the first floor window – veiled in long hair. A woman or a gaunt man, skin the colour of Cotswold stone. I checked the compass needle – I stood at the North wing – that window had no floor below it. The face moved away, its image stamped on my retinas. My limbs iced up, bad thoughts skulked my brain. None of the volunteers had access to the North tower. A set of keys is given to the caretaker during the winter months when the bats hibernate in St. John's church, I had the other set. Two large iron grilles must be unlocked to get to it, they kept people out and protect the bats. I heaved my body up the stairs, too tired to think. I hurried to reach a shimmer of white ahead in the gloom of the stairwell. Fabric trailed around the corners, like a net curtain or a christening gown. It escaped my fingers at every turn; I fell up the steps, running out of breath. In places the staircase opened out, steps gave way to nothing, floors and fireplaces hung over the abyss. I hated edging over the gratings underfoot, like those in church as a boy.

Stories leapt around my imagination, of the Victorian family, of Lady Blanche, the Leigh daughter I liked the most. There were no less than seven unexplained deaths during the construction of the mansion, hers included. Reaching the top of the tower and faced with a stronger strain of vertigo than I'd ever experienced, I could have sworn I'd be next. A solitary

Daubenton's bat clung to the wall. The wind whispered Vespers, Vespers and my pounding heart was reminded of the bat vigil. I picked him off and cradled him in my hands, tickled his underbelly, tagged his leg with a metal clip from my pocket, stroked his nose. Cold whirled up from the stairs and the bat's claws tore at me, wings unfurled and flailing. Even he couldn't stand to be near me. As he took wing, a milky shape dashed past, lace scratched my cheek bringing with it the acrid, burnt smell of shame. A figure stood up on the turret to my left, leaning into the night.

"No, stop!" I called.

It launched over the turret into the precipice, and like a veil fleshed out by air, went floating down. A trick, a distraction? Something else moved at the edge of the woods. I shone the torch out there, and stood glowing by the branches was the boy, still in his shorts, arm statically positioned towards the track, pointing away from this place, the way back to cars and pubs and home. I broke into a run, back down the stairs, slipping and falling, first on the stone, then gravel, then earth and roots. I found myself in a clearing, covered in bruises and scratches and gasping for air, unsure whether I was running away or towards something. The boy was nowhere to be seen. Bats soared over my pathetic form, on each side, trees mocked me. As I'd tell them all later, after that I didn't fancy sleeping alone.

I found Josie's tent quickly. Undid the zip one notch at a time, more when the cows mooed, as they muffled the noise. She was a waxwork of herself in perfect repose. She looked like Lady Blanche in the sepia-toned pictures I'd been pawing over. I could have touched her, held her close like the bat, but her little heart would have had such a fright if she'd woken up. I led down next to her on the edge of the teasingly unfastened sleeping bag, her breath on my face. Scared to move lest the horrors came for me or she stirred. Things I'd locked away clawed their way back – the sniggers of my Pet Superstore colleagues; Dr Hall's warning of blackouts, loss of memory, insomnia, delusions; a Labrador sliced open from gullet to spleen, intestines hanging out on the concrete. Screams punctuated my sleep and darkness took hold.

I wake under multicoloured flowers. She sleeps still in cold light. I'm coated in dew and the heaviness has lifted; I could walk for hours if I needed to. Perhaps I won't go home today, nature is bet-ter for me, I'm more myself here than in the city. Outside the tent, people talk in solemn tones. I crawl out. Old Alan, Carl are huddled together, the women are dabbing their eyes with hankies. They must be hanging after all that rum. In the periphery something so incongruous against the mansion wall, silver, blue and red: a police car parked in the mud.

"Ewen," says Alan, and shuffles over. Two policemen follow.

"We checked your tent and you weren't there," he explains.

"No, I …" I point to Josie's tent.

"Ewen Leisler, is it?"says the first policemen. "We want to ask you and your party a few questions and then you will have to vacate the site immediately."

"Why? We've done nothing wrong." I think of the empties of Captain Morgan by the fire.

"We have some very bad news. A body has been found in the woods. A young male child. Missing since yesterday lunchtime. We have reason to believe he was strangled. Is there anything of note that you can remember?"

I'm bolted to the ground. The silvery skin of his neck, the hair feathering on my hand. But I didn't touch him, though, did I?

"You're a bat enthusiast, is that right sir?"

Bat conservationist, I think, The Guardian of the Bats. I nod. "They're sleeping now."

And they're asking me more questions, about the Land Rover, time, who was with me, when. My hands are in my pockets, I don't know what else to do with them. I'm distracted by the thought of Josie, of possessing her as her throat crackled and her breath ebbed.

The other policeman approaches the flowery tent.

"Is there someone else in here?" he says. "Hello?"

The one in front of me frowns, "What's that you have there?"

I stand still, feel my eyeballs dart. Something prickles over me. The policeman pulls back the tent door.

The other looks over at him and back at me.

"What's in your pocket, sir?"

He takes hold of my arm, a rougher, more human touch than I'm used to. He unravels the red wool from my pocket, her scarf wrapped tightly around my hand.

THE VILLAGE BELOW

BY

MARIA J. PÉREZ CUERVO

WE REACHED the reservoir the morning of the festival, after hours of driving in the dark on the winding mountain road. From the flat, grey-green waters emerged the pointed tip of a tower, crowned by a cross. The landscape was almost unnaturally still, apart from three birds gliding above the tower, as if they were guarding what had been abandoned below.

"Eerie, isn't it?" the producer said as he slowed down. "These drowned villages always are."

"For all I know we could be in Wales." The presenter scratched his beard and yawned loudly. "They better have good Rioja."

The long journey had made us all cranky. After losing his patience when I'd taken the wrong turn, the producer had claimed the driver's seat, effortlessly finding the way as he discussed the newly appointed commissioning editor with the presenter.

Meanwhile, Bane and I kept quiet at the back. Judging from his breathing he'd managed to doze off. We had a long day of work ahead of us, and we all knew there wouldn't be any more time to sleep.

The new village was only five minutes away from the reservoir, a labyrinth of modest houses, all grey stone and slate roofs. Some locals were up already: a woman sweeping her doorway, two men on a rusty bench, staring at our van from under their flat caps. There was nothing territorial in their stare, but a certain resignation, a vague sadness that dulled the shine in their eyes like a thin layer of sawdust.

"So you're the English." At the

I THOUGHT I COULD HEAR THE BELLS RINGING, A QUIET, DROWNED SOUND THAT SEEMED TO COME FROM WITHIN A DREAM.

tavern, the woman behind the bar gave me a faint smile, glancing at my three colleagues, who had taken seats by the window and were already rowdier than anybody else. "Will you be here for long?"

"We're leaving tomorrow morning. Heading to France for another festival."

I had to raise my voice to be heard over their laughter. She turned towards them, and a deep line of worry appeared between her eyebrows.

"I don't think we've had anybody filming us since it was built," she said while she prepared our plates. Her hands were rough and cracked; the bar old but immaculate. Hanging behind her was a black and white portrait of a heavy-lidded boy of about eight, with an irregular fringe and a jacket too short in the sleeves. "It's been over fifty years now. I still remember them, talking about how good the regime was, helping us find another place."

There was bitterness in her words, still.

"You lived in the other village?" I asked.

"Until I was twelve."

"And then?"

She tightened her lips, seeming to disappear behind a mask of repressed anger, but soon resurfaced again.

"Then they told us we had to leave, so we came here. It was the least bad option. See them?" She jerked her chin at the other group in the far corner, four middle-aged men, drinking their coffee, reading the morning papers. "Most of them were born in the other village. The houses our parents built are underwater." Her voice turned into a sibilant whisper. "Some family members are still there, buried in the graveyard by the church. We all left something behind, yet we'll never be able to return."

The question formed clearly in my mind. Was he your brother? I don't know what made me keep it to myself. The portrait of the boy was directly in front of me, but it was the producer's glare in the corner of my eye that made me react.

"Would you be happy to talk to camera?" I asked instead. She nodded, but later, when Bane pointed the camera at her, she grew shy, the silence between her words dense.

In the afternoon, hundreds of villagers, some coming from places nearby, plodded to the reservoir, their gazes locked on the tarmac. Men squinting into the weak light, women with their arms entwined, children waving rosemary twigs.

The priest and the two altar boys were on the first line, surrounded by the villagers, all mesmerised by the motorboat advancing into the water. The dark shapes of two scuba divers disappeared in the grey-green mass and we were left with the monotonous voice of the priest concatenating blessings. When the scuba divers returned, the crowd gave a round of applause. It

sounded sorrowful, funereal, but its tail end merged into a sound of a different kind. I held my breath and listened. It was a young, mercurial, mischievous laughter. A girl with a candy-striped dress laughed in delight, suddenly the focus of all gazes. A nervous hand clasped her shoulder; a woman, her mother, quickly leant down until her lips brushed her ear. Whatever she told the child made her look down, pouting, blending again into the despair of the crowd.

Eight villagers guarded the platform where the divers were now placing the saint. The algae had given his face a greenish pallor, but they grew thicker and darker in the hollows of his eyes. The bearers lifted his throne, slowly marching up the road, and the villagers followed in a procession. "They need him down below," an old man told the camera, pointing at the water with his gnarled hand, "but today we take him out and we remember." Among the whispers, I thought I could hear the

bells ringing, a quiet, drowned sound that seemed to come from within a dream.

"Thank God it's over," said the presenter once we were back in the tavern for dinner. "For Christ's sake, B., you couldn't have brought us to a more depressing place. Festival? Felt like a bloody funeral. I thought these people knew how to have fun."

"But they do! Do you remember the last time we were in Spain, Bane?" The producer poured more red wine in his glass. "East coast, somewhere called – I don't remember. Now that was fun."

Dinner was a hearty stew, as dark as the red wine. We drank three bottles, but I still had to force myself to smile as they reminisced of previous shoots. Bane looked at me a few times, and I knew he saw through me. "You want to keep your job, kid?" he'd told me only a few weeks ago. "Then you do your thing well, you get drunk with the producer and you laugh at his jokes. That's all there is." And so I tried, even though I didn't even know if I cared.

By midnight we were the only ones left in the room, apart from the owner. "We need spirits," the producer decided, turning to me. "Do you mind getting a bottle from her?"

The woman had spent the last hour mopping the floor and tidying up the tables, and now she was cleaning the bar. I asked her for a bottle of gin, but she shook her head.

"We're closing down."

Secretly relieved, I cleared the bill and thanked her. Her expression seemed different now: the line of worry between her eyebrows had returned. "Be careful on your way back," she said.

"Wolves?"

"The dead." Her voice became a whisper. "They like the company. The night of the festival — they sense the warmth and the joy of the living. They get hungry."

When we were out on the street, the crickets chirping, the smell of burnt rosemary still lingering in the air, the darkness was deeper than in any city, and a jolt of primal fear clenched my stomach. I walked faster, leading the way, but a loud thump made me stop and look back. The presenter was on his knees, and the three of them were trying to stifle their laughs. Bane shushed the others, but he couldn't keep a straight face.

The breeze brought a distinctive smell, wet leaves and petrichor, and a shadow seemed to fall upon the street. I noticed then the lonely figure moving slowly towards us, short and unsteady.

"Let's go," I mumbled, extending a hand to the presenter, but they didn't seem to notice. The figure was just ten feet away, its features now visible. It had eyes as dark as the saint's, a jacket short in the arms and an irregular fringe. The way it walked, like something that had been asleep for decades, made my blood freeze. I stumbled back and saw the rest, the legion of shadows that followed the boy, cold, emaciated, ravenous.

I'd always heard that fear makes you fight or flee, but my limbs didn't respond. I must have fallen, because I found myself curled up on the floor, shivering. I covered my head and my ears with my arms and closed my eyes tightly, as a damp cold ran over me and a fetid smell made my stomach churn. It's over, I thought. This was to be my resting place, and despite the horror I felt a strange relief.

I became aware of a soft murmur, a hand on my shoulder. When I opened my eyes again I saw the face of a man, vaguely familiar, in the morning light. He asked if I was all right, and I recognised the dull sound of the priest's voice.

They found their bodies floating in the reservoir. The coroner confirmed there was alcohol in their blood and the official verdict was accidental death. "They sense the warmth and the joy of the living," she'd said.

I believe it was my despair that saved me.

THE NIGHT OF THE FESTIVAL — THEY SENSE THE WARMTH AND THE JOY OF THE LIVING. THEY GET HUNGRY.

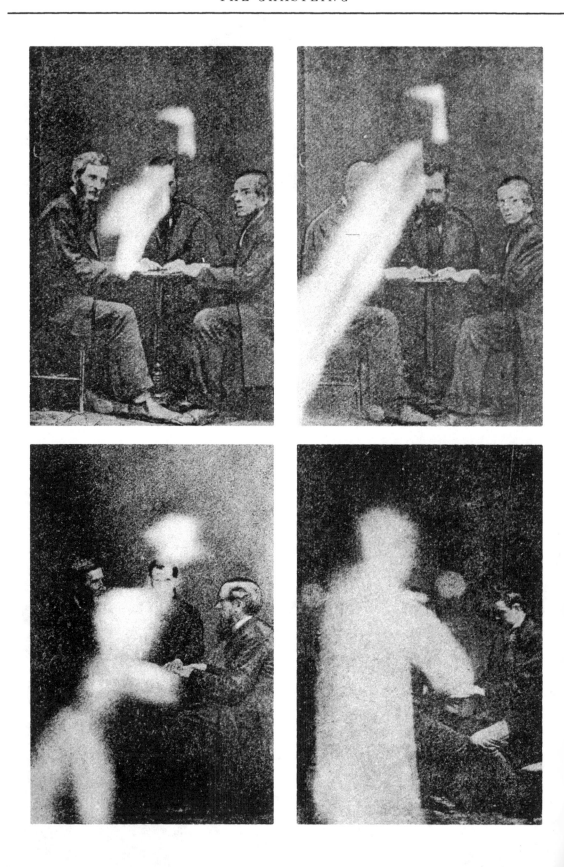

BY LEONA PRESTON

CALLING THE DEAD

BY

LOUISE LLOYD

ON THE DAY of the funeral the weather was stormy. The yew trees at the border of the cemetery shivered and moaned in the wind. A handful of mourners battled with black umbrellas and rain churned the graveside to mud. Rachel could feel the wind shoving at her back as if it wanted to push her into the open grave. She watched as the coffin was lowered into the earth.

"…ashes to ashes, dust to dust…" The gale carried the vicar's voice away into the roaring sky. The funeral director's men stood with their heads bowed, impervious to the squalls of rain. One of them trickled a handful of dry earth onto the coffin's glistening surface. The wind screamed and snatched the order of service from Rachel's numb fingers. It fluttered away across the sodden grass. She shivered. Rain had soaked through the shoulders of her good black coat and she could feel the cold mud through the thin soles of her best shoes.

As soon as the vicar had taken her hands and mouthed some platitudes he hurried back to the church. Rachel stood looking down into the grave, barely noticing Julia's aunt and cousins saying goodbye and running for their cars.

What if there had been a mistake?

What if she wasn't dead?

The thought went round and round in her head like a tune she couldn't stop hearing. She turned to leave, realised she was alone. The rain was easing now and the yew trees were a dark livid green against the bruise coloured sky.

The house was quiet. Rachel put the radio on for company but after a few minutes the music and shrill voices made her head ache and she switched it off again. Now the only sound was the ticking of the clock above the fireplace. She picked up her book but found she was reading the same sentence over and over until it made no sense. Outside the streetlamp had come on. The night stepped closer and pressed against the window. As she shut the curtains something moved out in the

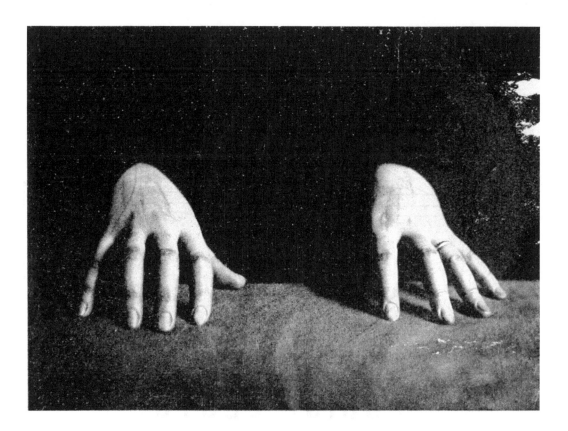

wet dark, a shadowed figure ducking out of sight. Rachel jumped and put her face to the glass. Just the wind shaking the hedge and the street light throwing crazy shadows.

She lay awake for a long time. Outside the wind had risen. It wailed around the eaves like a fairground ghost train and drove rain against the window. Across the landing Julia's room was still full of her things. Rachel had been in once to choose Julia's burial outfit. Her friend's absence was almost a presence. It was as though she had just left the room for a minute and would come back and ask Rachel what she was doing in her wardrobe. Rachel closed her eyes and saw again the gleaming surface of the coffin and heard the dry gritting sound of dry earth hitting the lid. The vicar reciting "...in sure and certain hope of the resurrection to eternal life..." The wind snatching the words of the burial service from his mouth. The rain on the flowers she had brought, their petals turned to sodden tissue paper. Julia in her coffin, under the earth. Her face pale and composed, her eyes shut.

Were they shut?

She pushed the thought away. Julia was gone and nothing would bring her back. She thought of the board and the glass in Julia's room and pushed that thought away too. Such things were not to be thought of when she was here alone and the wind howled. The memories came though, just the same. The room lit by a single candle. She and Julia with their fingers resting on the glass. The pale oval of Julia's face, calm and priestess like as she called for the dead. Rachel turned her head restlessly from side to side as she tried in vain to dislodge the memories. She didn't want to remember. The atmosphere in Julia's room was always different after the sessions. The air was thick and oppressive and the sense of being stared at was overwhelming.

Rachel shook her head again and sat up. It was ridiculous to go on like this. She would get up and make a warm drink. She got out of bed and reached for her dressing gown. She was on the landing when a door closed quietly downstairs. She froze with her hand halfway to the light switch. Had she really heard that? She let her hand fall back to her side and stood in the dark, listening to the wind shriek murderously outside. She should go down and check there were no windows open. She went to the top of the stairs, aware that she was

IT CARRIED WITH IT A SMELL OF CARRION. OF SOMETHING LEFT TOO LONG AND BEGINNING TO DECAY.

moving slowly. She had forgotten her slippers and her feet were already cold. She took one step down and stopped. The hall was a well of darkness and a black tide seemed to be creeping up the stairs towards her. She wanted to retreat before it but forced herself down another two steps.

An icy draught cut her ankles and she remembered the cold currents of air that swirled around Julia's room when they used the board. Once there had been dragging footsteps on the landing and a heavy blow on the bedroom door. Rachel wept with terror and Julia had laughed. She called for the visitor to go away, that she revoked her invitation. Dragging footsteps faded away across the landing and Julia had looked at her with triumph and, Rachel thought, scorn.

Don't think about it, she told herself. Her imagination was trying to frighten her and she would not let it. She made herself creep down another two steps. The blackness in the hall was a solid, inky thing that she was afraid of, but compelled to enter. Her hearing felt supernaturally alert and her eyes strained into the blackness of the hall but could see nothing. There was a sound, then. A soft, barely there sigh of a sound. Like the brush of a bare foot across the floor or someone pushing the air ahead of them as they moved. Rachel felt terror grip her like an old enemy. Her heart was beating fast in her throat as she slid another step down into the encroaching black tide. Outside she could hear the wind chuckling and muttering like a madman. She took another step and another. The cold was creeping up her legs beneath her thin nightdress. She spoke into the darkness in a shaking whisper;

"Julia?"

From the deepest shadow came a grating, mirthless giggle. Rachel was aware of swooning terror and at the same time a feeling of

irrational relief. I knew she wasn't dead. The thought pushed everything else away. I knew it was a mistake. Her feet took her down the last half dozen stairs. The hall was bone chilling cold. The tiles beneath her feet were shards of ice leading into frozen blackness. She put out a trembling hand.

"Julia?"

Again came the shrill giggle. It carried with it a smell of carrion. Of something left too long and beginning to decay. Rachel felt the last shred of reason leave her and she gave it up gladly. "Julia?" she said again and this time a voice answered her. A voice cracked and gritting with disuse and dirt.

"Darling" Julia said. And a shadow detached itself from the blacker shadows behind it. She was wearing the dress Rachel had chosen and there was wet mud caked on her shoes. She was smiling at Rachel but it was it was as if the muscles of her face had forgotten the movements. Her eyes were sunken in her white face, and the thin skin around them bruised deep purple. She smelled like wet earth and the undertaker's preservative and beneath both of these was a whiff of sweet, black rot.

"Darling?" She held out a hand and Rachel saw that her nails were broken and filthy, rimed with earth. Julia had always been so careful about her nails. Manicures and polish. Hand lotion and cotton gloves. Her slim, elegant fingers on the glass as it slid across the board. She looked into Julia's face again and Julia took a clumsy step towards her.

"Darling, I didn't know where I was. I was lost in the dark and it was so cold…"

Rachel took an involuntary step back. Some deep, atavistic part of her brain that usually lay asleep was awake and hammering at her consciousness.

"Rachel?" Julia's heels scraped the tiles as

GO BACK.
YOU'RE DEAD
YOU DON'T BELONG HERE.

she moved towards her. "Darling, let's go upstairs and we'll get the board out."

Rachel shook her head. "No. No you shouldn't be here." She felt the bottom stair against her calves and stepped back onto it. Julia's face changed. The smile became snarling bared teeth. Her eyes were dark and baleful. "You always were a coward, weren't you, Rachel? Always snivelling and afraid…" As she spat the last word Julia clutched the hand rail and pulled herself towards the stairs. Rachel began to back up the stairs. The deep swooning terror and sensation of unreality had vanished. She felt alert and clear headed. The thing that had been Julia began to climb after her. The smell of decay and wet earth was stronger and Rachel gagged and covered her nose and mouth with her arm. Julia's broken fingernails scrabbled at the bannister as she dragged herself up another step.

"Cowardly, stupid Rachel." Julia giggled, a high shrill screeching giggle that hurt Rachel's ears. "Stupid, pathetic Rachel…"

This thing wasn't Julia. Julia had been proud, arrogant sometimes but never deliberately unkind.

"No" Rachel said, her voice steady. "That's not how it was."

The Julia thing looked at her and cocked its head. "No?" It sneered and with horror Rachel heard her own voice coming from its blackening lips.

"Oh Rachel you're my best friend. Don't leave me alone. What will I do without you?" Another shrill grating giggle.

"No" Rachel said again. "Julia, go back. You have to go back to sleep."

She made herself look into the black eyes that were shining with spite and hate. Somewhere deep inside them was a vestige of the real Julia and she looked sad, confused and desperately tired.

"Julia." Rachel said, and this time her voice

shook a little. "Go back. You're dead. You don't belong here."

Julia pulled herself up another step. "The dead pull the living down, Rachel." Her voice cracked and wavered. "When you call for the dead, they all come. Did you know that?"

"Go back," Rachel whispered. "Go back." Then she remembered Julia at one of the board sessions. The dragging footsteps. The heavy blow on the door. She took a deep breath and took her arm away from her face.

"I revoke my invitation."

The wind screamed and slammed against the side of the house. Julia's mouth opened and she uttered a choked, whistling gasp. She held out a hand, filthy with grave dirt, to Rachel and this time it was the real Julia looking up at her.

"Rachel, I love you. I'm sorry…"

Her friend's face was just as she remembered, just for a second. Then she was gone and there was nothing but a handful of golden dust motes dancing on the dim staircase. Somewhere downstairs a door slammed and made Rachel jump. All the strength went out of her and she sat down on the stairs and began to weep.

She sat there until the wind gradually ceased and the sky was light. Then she lit the fire and when it was blazing, she pushed the board into it. She broke the glass in the back yard, and buried the fragments with salt.

When she had done these things Rachel put on her good black coat and her best shoes and went to see the estate agent on the high street. He promised to send a man to put up the "For Sale" sign that afternoon.

Exhaustion hit her as she closed the front door. She hung up her coat and eased her feet from the confining shoes. She looked at the stairs and saw the clumps of mud and grass trodden into the carpet. From the shadowed landing came a faint giggle.

MOTH

BY

LYNN HARDAKER

THE LAST THING I wanted that night was to meet anyone. And that was certainly the last thing I expected, considering it was well after midnight and the cemetery gate had been locked for hours. All I had with me was my backpack, so hopping the fence should have been easy, but even with a good effort, I landed awkwardly next to a bush. The weather was unusually good for the city in the dead of summer: hot without being humid or too smoggy. And the air in the cemetery was cool and scented with some type of night flower that I didn't know. It was nice, but didn't do anything to lift my mood. I didn't want to spend the night in a hostel or shelter. I didn't want the noise of other people around me, so this seemed like the ideal place.

It's a huge cemetery. Acres and acres right in the middle of the city. Last stop for some of the more notable residents and families over the past century and a half. Filled with Ancient Greek styled mausoleums with names carved above them; names now associated with department stores, or communications companies, or beer.

It was a clear night with a bright, full moon. I made my way fairly easily between the gravestones. The deeper in I went, the quieter it got. I decided to stop for a bit.

Sitting down with my back against a gravestone, I lit a cigarette and pulled out a mickey of cheap whiskey. I still felt numb. It was a numbness that had been growing for years. A cocoon of sort, built up layer by layer. I took another swig and turned my thoughts to where I was.

I've never been one to let my imagination run wild, but as I sat there, the gentle burn of store-bought booze sliding down my throat, I kept imagining the bodies in the earth below me. Dozens and dozens of them. Just lying there, some for the better part of a century. What would they look like now, I started to wonder, feeling a chill shudder through me. Dead. It was one thing to think about no longer existing, something I did on an hourly basis; and an entirely different thing to think about being a corpse.

I couldn't stand the thought of sitting there any longer and was about to get up, when I saw her. At first I thought it was a shadow, or some trick of the dark. But before I knew it, she was standing right in front of me. For half a second, I was too shocked to react. She stared down at me with an intense, unwavering gaze. I stood. In spite of having a good foot, and probably fifty pounds on her, I felt uneasy. I smiled weakly.

"Hi," I said. The word sounded oddly inadequate. The girl cocked her head. She seemed to be sizing me up, so I did the same to her. She

looked young, bit younger than me, maybe early twenties. She wore dark, loose fitting pants and one of those baggy poet shirts. Her black hair was long and pulled back from her face, her skin so pale it almost glowed under the moon's light. The most impressive thing about her features were her eyes: large and intense, with that 'old soul' quality. It was clear that she didn't feel at all threatened by me.

After staring for longer than was either comfortable or polite, her expression changed. It became one of pity. What was she able to see in me, I wondered; not much liking the thought. I looked down, unable to hold her stare.

"You're welcome to stay with us tonight," she said simply. My first impulse was to decline. I had chosen this place in order to be alone. To be quiet. To try to get reacquainted with who I was, since I didn't seem to have a clue anymore. Though, to be honest, I didn't know if it was even worth the bother.

But after a few seconds, the thought of being with someone who wasn't a fellow prisoner or a guard started to appeal. Maybe I'd been craving normal human contact more than I cared to admit. More than I thought I deserved.

I took another slug of whiskey, capped it, and stuffed it back in my backpack.

"Thanks. That would be nice."

I followed her, noticing that she wasn't wearing shoes. It got darker as we delved into the heart of the cemetery. Trees clustered thickly together, like gigantic hands blocking the sky from my view. She didn't have to look down to pick her way past the uneven mounds of earth and the flat grave markers hidden by overgrown grass, their corners sticking up, ready to catch a toe. My eyes strained to find the way.

It did occur to me briefly that this might be some sort of trap, but my instincts had been honed and I didn't sense any danger. Weirdness, yes, but not danger.

After walking a few minutes, she stopped at one of the mausoleums. I shouldn't have been surprised. Where else could you sleep, hidden in a place like that. For a moment, she hesitated, her hand on the door handle. I thought she might be about to change her mind, wondering whether it was such a good idea to invite a strange man into her squat. And I certainly wouldn't blame her if she had.

But she didn't. She pushed the door open. It made a sound of stone grinding against stone. My heart started to hammer. We entered. The girl shut the door and I looked around. The room was larger that it should have been. The walls were lined with stone shelves. On each shelf was a stone casket with a name engraved along its side. There were two upholstered armchairs with a low, wooden table between them. Someone was sitting in one of the armchairs, staring at the casket in front of them. Every hair on my neck prickled to life. The person turned toward me.

I didn't know what I was expecting, but it wasn't a middle aged woman. I smiled and when she returned the smile, her face was transformed.

"Hello," she said in a brittle voice. The skin around her eyes crinkled with smile wrinkles. She was quite lovely, radiant. I felt a little embarrassed. She was easily old enough to be my mother. Slowly, however, her smile faded and it was as though she was visibly fading. I thought she must be sick, but then this was hardly a place for a sick woman to be living.

The girl went over and knelt at the woman's side. She whispered something. For a second, I wondered if it could be her mother, but that seemed unlikely. They didn't look anything alike and there was something in their manner toward one another that didn't seem like that of a mother and daughter.

The only light in the room came from what I at first thought were lanterns hanging from brackets in the walls, but I soon realized were cages. In each one was a huge moth, its wings and body glowing with a light that was as cool and silvery as moonlight. I was mesmerized by them. But their eerie, unnatural glow made me feel uneasy.

I walked over to the one closest to me. I raised my hand to it. It moved toward me. Quickly, I pulled away. Afraid. Though I didn't know why.

"You can sit if you want," she girl said, nodding to the empty chair. I took a closer look at the woman sitting in the other one. She had gone back to just staring at the casket. I stared at it too, but could find no words. I went closer to the girl.

"Is she... is she alright?"

The girl stared at me. I was determined to hold her stare, but again I found myself looking away.

"She is just as she wishes to be."

There was bitterness in her voice. She went around to the cages, looking in at the moths almost as though they were pets. I was really tired and part of me just wanted to sit in the chair and nap, but I was too curious about this unlikely pair and their strange dwelling. I wondered why the girl had invited me in.

I watched her, curious about the way she moved her lips as though she was saying something to each of them. The woman didn't seem to notice or care. There was a sadness to the woman now that was so at odds with how she'd seemed when she'd greeted me. It hit me stronger than it should have. My throat felt the squeeze that comes before crying. I cleared my throat. The woman was starting to unsettle me.

The girl turned around, as if in answer to my uneasiness. That look of pity crossed her face again.

"You are so... torn," she said. "By what you did. And what was done to you."

I stood up. She was hitting close to the truth and I didn't like it. A swell of anger rose in me. I swallowed it down.

"I don't know what you're talking about," I lied. She stared at me. This time, perhaps due to my annoyance, I was able to meet her gaze. After a moment in which it felt as though she'd read every thought and feeling and memory I'd ever had, she looked over at the woman. Once again I had that feeling that she was coming to a decision about something.

"We're all prisoners, aren't we?" she said and walked to the door, opened it and went out. Too shaken to respond, I followed her. I noticed that she'd picked something up on her way out. A cage, like the ones containing the moths.

It was a relief to be outside after the stifling air of the mausoleum. We didn't walk far, before she stopped at a new grave. A mound of freshly turned earth piled on top of it, filling the air with a damp, loamy smell that reminded me of childhood.

She clambered onto it and knelt down. I was not liking this. She held the cage out in front of her and started whispering something. If they were actual words, they were from no language I'd ever heard before.

And then, slowly at first, the air between the grave and the cage began to shimmer. It was as though it was filled with thousands of tiny insects. With an almost liquid movement, the tiny particles moved toward each other and congealed into a form.

The girl opened the door to the cage and let the newly formed moth flutter inside. Quickly, she closed it and slid the latch into place. Her face shone eerily in the moth's cool glow. She looked over at me. I felt dizzy.

"What..." I couldn't finish the question.

"When a person dies, their life force, soul, whatever you choose to call it, leaves their body." Her voice was so calm, it gave me goosebumps.

"But sometimes there are the smallest bits left behind. Scraps, fragments."

I stared at the moth, feeing slightly sick.

"But why do you catch them? Imprison them?" I couldn't pull my eyes from the moth, from what not very long ago had been part of the life force of a person.

"It's what I do. What I've always done. I'm called a soul-collector. One of the last, I suppose. Perhaps the very last." The light from the moth made her features sharper. She looked so young, yet now I understood the ageless look in her eyes. This was no girl. And that was no moth.

"Why are they being kept captive in the mausoleum?"

"You don't like the idea of things being kept captive, do you."

"No, I don't. Five years in prison will do that to a person."

"But you deserved it. Even you think so."

I couldn't decide which was worse: her

soul-collecting or her mind-reading. I didn't like either.

"No offense," I said, "but it's not really any of your business."

"Of course it's not."

She held the cage up higher and stared into it. "But," she continued, looking at the moth not at me, "you will stay in your own prison until you forgive yourself."

I almost walked off. I wasn't in the mood for psycho-babble. But something made me stay. She held the cage out to me. The moth fluttered erratically. I found myself leaning away from it.

"Come," she said, "hold it."

I shook my head. There was no way.

"Why do you take them?" I asked again. Her face looked pained.

"I don't like what I do with them, what she does with them," she said softly, "but I'm bound to her."

"The woman?"

She nodded. That explained her bitterness toward the older woman, but didn't explain what they did with the moths.

"But why don't you just stop? Tell her you don't want to do whatever it is you do with them anymore."

She gave a wistful smile.

"I have no choice. I need her just as she needs me. Our bond was created years ago. Probably before even your grandparents were born."

It was all too much. It was difficult enough to get my head around being free and returning to the world I knew before, but to have to confront this was too much. I half wondered if I was hallucinating, if I'd finally gone mad. But since this was my current reality, whether in madness or sanity or god knows what, I had to go with it.

"What are you telling me? That you and that woman are, what, a hundred years old?" My skin prickled as I spoke the words, instinctively knowing I'd come close to a truth.

"She and I are bound by old ties."

"Magic."

"Yes, magic. She's was quite an accomplished witch in her time. She managed to find me, and learned about the soul fragments."

"But why did you collect them?"

"I, and others like me, have always done so. We gather them and free them. If they stay, the part of soul that has already left will not be able to find its final rest. And that causes problems. Wandering spirits. Ghosts carrying fear, frustration,

anger."

"But that's not what you're doing now. You're trapping them. You admitted that."

She smiled. Not happily.

"Yes. Now I trap them. For her. They keep her alive; keep her from aging. She wove a strong magic, a spell of her own. Quite ingenious, really."

The woman should have died years, generations ago. I pictured her. Her face so beautiful and alive when she smiled, but instantly transformed back into something grey and lifeless when she didn't. Sitting there all day, all night staring at... at the remains of her family. A living hell. Of her own making.

"You can't leave, can you," I asked.

She shook her head.

"It's part of the binding."

"And if you do leave?"

"I die."

I said nothing. She continued.

"Which I've been tempted to do on so many occasions. I don't have to tell you about that feeling."

I nodded. Now I understood her comment about the three of us being prisoners. I took a deep breath.

"But the people, I mean the souls... it's not really for you and her to decide what happens to them."

"It wasn't for you to decide what happened to the soul of the man you killed, was it."

It wasn't a question. It was a well aimed shot. I exhaled loudly.

"No. Of course not. And I've been beating myself up every minute of every day ever since."

"Even though it wasn't entirely your fault. Even though you've served your sentence. Paid your debt."

I shook my head and looked down. I didn't want to discuss it. Not with her, not with the shrink in the prison, not with anyone.

"You've not been beating yourself up, you've been slowly killing yourself. Killing every scrap of humanity left in you. Why? As punishment?"

I put my hand up. I wanted her to stop.

"You're still a prisoner," she said.

I looked up. My vision was blurred and it took me a second to realize that it was because of tears. I wiped them away, not caring whether she noticed. My mind was reeling with all she'd said, and with all she'd seen in me. I was overwhelmed by a sudden flooding of emotions.

I didn't want to cry, but the tears came. I

couldn't remember the last time I'd been able to let them out. We stayed like that for a few minutes, a strange montage: me – standing and silently crying, her – kneeling on a fresh grave with a glowing moth in a cage.

Finally, the tears slowed. It was strange, and liberating, not to feel the least bit embarrassed about them. She was looking at me. Her face unreadable. But I knew what I had to do.

I took the cage from her and walked back to the mausoleum. I heard her following behind. When I entered, the woman turned to me. She smiled that enchanting smile again. I almost lost my resolve.

I started with the moth in the cage I was holding, unlatching the door and pulling it open. Immediately the moth flew out. After that, I went from one cage to the next.

I was behind her now. The woman turned herself around, her hands digging into the back of the armchair, lifting herself as well as she could with those atrophied limbs, to watch me.

"No. No, you must stop. Stop!"

It was difficult to steel myself against her cries, but I had to tell myself, not that she'd done something wrong and deserved punishment, rather that this was a way of freeing her. Freeing the girl. Freeing me. None of it made any sense, but I knew in my gut that this was what I had to do.

One by one the moths flew out of their cages. The woman's hands were on her cheeks, her mouth set in a noiseless cry. The girl was standing by the door, watching the woman, a complicated mix of emotions on her face.

When the last moth was free, the girl walked out the door. The moths followed and I came

behind them. I was expecting the woman to appear, but she didn't. The almost inaudible sound of weeping came from within the mausoleum. I closed my eyes against it and followed the glowing path of moths.

The girl stopped and the moths spun and swirled in beautiful patterns in the air above her. She raised her arms and they dipped down to make contact with her, then fluttered away again. She looked at me. It was a direct look which made me feel a rush of joy. And made me want to cry. Her skin began to shimmer, to glow. It began a fluttering movement and seconds later, her body pulled apart into dozens, hundreds of glowing moths.

It was the most beautiful thing I'd ever experienced. The moths of her body slowly moved upward and joined the dance with the others. Together they swirled higher and higher. Then all at once, they separated and flew off in different directions, disappearing into the sky.

I breathed in the scent of those night flowers and watched until the last moth was long gone from my vision and dawn began to bleed into the sky. Slowly, I walked back to the mausoleum. I felt duty bound to do so.

Inside, it looked just as it should have. No chairs, no table, no woman. Just the musty smell of age and mould and rot. I went to the casket the woman had been staring at. There was a name on it now: Miranda Thompson. I ran my fingers along the letters.

After a moment, I shouldered my backpack and walked out. The first birds were starting to sing. That was a sound I hadn't heard for a long while. I smiled, just a little, as I made my way toward the fence.

THE TOWER

BY

MATT HOPKINS

I, *Jean-Pierre Jourdain*, must tell you of this tale from my past, and I beg your indulgence; many of the affairs of my long life are unfinished and unexplained, and these writings concern one of them. As the Lord is my witness, all of this account is the truth. Only you, of all my friends and family, have the experience and wisdom in these matters to accept what I now write.

I was a young man as this story begins, full of joy, and the spirit of adventure was upon me. It was the summer of 1789, and among the growing unrest within the Kingdom, I had foolishly decided to travel many miles to the north some weeks before, leaving my father, mother and younger sister in the small chateau that was my birthplace and home. In those days I was easy with money; a gambler, fond of leisure and a lover of women, and

there seemed no reason for a dark haired, bright eyed fellow not to enjoy his life to the full. So I rode far and wide across the rolling hills and meadows of my beloved France.

Upon returning, I was dusty and weary upon my horse and glad to be close to home once more. But upon entering the tree lined avenue which led to our property, I saw a thin wisp of smoke beyond the low rise ahead, in the direction of our vineyards. The smell of burning wood was in the warm air. Reining in, I listened and heard a faint crackling in the distance. I felt a knot of fear in the pit of my stomach for my loved ones, as I remembered the baying mob in a village square I had barely outrun a few days before... as I began to spur my mare onwards in haste, a figure came tumbling out of the hedge-row to the right of the road and righted

IT LOOMED OUT OF THE SHIFTING MISTS, AND IN THE TWILIGHT IT WAS LIKE A VAST SKELETAL FINGER THRUST FROM GROUND TO SKY.

itself before my startled mount. It was old Charles, a servant of my family. "Seigneur, Seigneur!" he cried out breathlessly, clutching at my reins with fear in his dark eyes beneath a furrowed brow. I had known the man since I was an infant, and I was distressed to see him in such poor condition. I asked him what the trouble was. "The workers have risen up, here and elsewhere across the province. There are many trouble makers, come here from far away to stir them up. Chateau Fleurie is burned to the ground... No, no, Seigneur, do not fear! they are safe! a friend of Seigneur Jourdain's, the merchant... M. Coronne?... he gave them warning, but none too soon. The master and his wife and your sister have fled, trying to reach La Rochelle with him..." As our hurried conversation went on, it seemed that he had waited for my return and watched for me from the hilltop to the east of the Chateau for five days since. He told me that it was no longer safe for me here, and that revolutionaries still prowled the ruins of my home. With a sinking heart, I cursed myself silently for my absence. I knew I must disguise myself, and follow my family to the sea if I could.

Charles and I travelled after dark to his home, where his wife kindly provided me with a meal (which I ate swiftly), and then found me some rough peasant clothes to replace my fine linen waistcoat, jacket and hose; a battered tricorne completed the outfit. My good riding boots I kept, for I knew how far it was to the

coast. Then, giving my faithful friend three silver Livre for gratitude and for his family, I bade him a sad farewell and set off to the west. There was anger in my heart at the thought of what may happen to my loved ones in the name of justice and I knew that I would never see my home again.

For several days I rode on, resting at weather beaten village taverns when I felt safe, and as my purse grew lighter, I spent more time sleeping in barns or roadside ditches in my rude clothes and ragged brown cloak. The misty night air was often cold in the rocky, tree shrouded hills, despite the season at hand. And always I thought of my family and their peril, and my right hand would seek the hilt of my sword, and my hunger and aching bones and soiled garments would fade in my mind before my fear for them.

And then, late one afternoon, the ground began to rise and the trees began to thin. A stark range of mountains rose up before me against the darkening sky, through which (I had been told by a traveller) there was a low pass. I soon came to a fork in the road (of this I had not been informed). So, choosing the wider of the two ways, I travelled on. After hours spent climbing a lonely, stony path up a winding mountainside, I began to doubt both the choosing of my route and my wisdom in not setting up camp before attempting to cross these crags. I considered my options, and it was clear to me that I could not retrace my climb in the fading twilight. So I urged my faithful horse onwards.

After a time I reached the summit, and came across a country I had never seen before; a kind of high moor, sparse of tree and bush. It was still, and cold - unnaturally so. A mist lay all around, wisps spreading from numerous small hollows in the boggy ground, so that distance and shape were hard to fix in the gloaming. The footing became treacherous for my horse, who stumbled and snorted, so I dismounted and walked, leading the mare by the reins. I felt a chill that numbed me to the bones as I trudged wearily on, and I pulled my cloak tighter as a sense of unease crept upon me. And then, as I began to fear exposure and encroaching darkness, I saw it before me.

A tower.

It loomed out of the shifting mists, and in the twilight it was like a vast skeletal finger thrust from ground to sky. Its aspect was ancient and badly ruined. It was round, perhaps 60 feet tall and half as much wide, flat topped and crumbling, a black silhouette before the dark purple clouds. Not a sign of life or light, and no sound came from it. Here there was no sound at all: not a bird, not an insect; my horse trembled by my side (and she was a brave beast). Even the air was utterly still. As if the scene held its breath, waiting for something to happen... I shook my head, and the curious feeling was gone. Now all I could think of was sleep and shelter for the night. As I wondered where the entrance to the tower might be, I spied a dark line ahead; a low, craggy masonry wall, square in shape and surrounding the tower. It was around 200 feet to a side and more than twice the height of a tall man, many stones having split and fallen away to leave several large cracks amid heaps of rubble. With the last light of day I tied my nervous horse to a nearby stunted tree, and climbed through the nearest fissure.

It was a garden. Or had once been; it was all overgrown but with a thin, twisted form of vegetation. Here on my left were the remains of an orchard gone wild, but bearing no fruit at all on their greyish withered boughs; around the knotted trunk of one of the further trees I saw what appeared to be white animal bones in the long ragged grass. Shallow pools lay scattered, and the smell of them was of rotted weeds. Now the clouds suddenly parted and the moon sailed into view above the tower, casting a pale blue-grey light that limned the scene before me. I walked cautiously on, watching, listening for signs of life: but silence was all around me, and brooding darkness was the edifice ahead. My feeling of foreboding and imminence returned, and the strangeness of the place unnerved me. Deciding to examine the tower, I moved cautiously across the damp earth. To my right were the twined stalks of long dead vines trailing upon the ground. In a slight depression I chanced upon a cracked and fallen sundial – covered in moss and fungus as to be hardly discernable. I looked up, and saw a dark archway to the right side of the tower that stood out in stark relief in the slanting moonbeams. I headed towards it. Only to be confronted by a sudden movement in the air: a shrieking and flapping sound and a shadowy shape passed across my vision. Startled at the noise, I threw my arms up in front of me but too late, a sharp pain lanced across my cheek. I looked wildly around but there was nothing now save a faint, receding chittering noise. I felt my face, and looking down saw with perfect clarity three drops of my own blood fall slowly, ever so slowly to the ground. I stood in a trance, the droplets glowing like rubies in the spectral light.

They fell upon a patch of bare earth.

There was the merest impression of an almost silent breath outward, and of a single faint heartbeat. And then in an instant it was all gone, as if a spell had been broken. The sense of foreboding was even stronger than before. I heard a soft scraping, rattling sound from near the trees, then sinister silence once more. Then there came a whinnying from my mare beyond the wall and the sound of her breaking tether and galloping away. Gone, and with her, my pack.

I went quickly to the archway, glancing fearfully at the sky in case of a further attack by my unseen assailant. In doing so I took in the rough stones of the tower at close hand. The archway itself was peaked and gothic. There were small openings in the wall at various heights, all of which were blackened and broken. I looked back at the entrance. The door was intact and heavy and made of a rusty iron riveted wood so blackened it resembled coal. There was a rusted iron keyhole at the middle. I knocked on the portal, hearing a hollow echo from within, I waited. There came no answer. I pressed against the door. It moved not an inch. I threw my weight against it twice, jarring my shoulder, then slumped forward in despair.

But something caught the corner of my eye: It was a large stone object, rectangular and part broken, lying some 20 feet further away to the right side of the tower. Though I was sure that no such thing was there when first I looked. Some instinct told me to go towards it, and as I did, I saw that it was a tomb, with several seemingly older structures beyond. It was greatly overgrown with sickly weeds and lichen. The lid was cracked and missing along the top third of its length, and any inscription had long been worn away by time. Now, not being a superstitious man, I was surprised at how much courage I had to muster to look within. I smelled earth, but of remains there was no sign. Then I noticed something give a dull glint in the ghostly light. I reached in and grasped it: a key. Of all the things to find in that place. It was a large, corroded key of what appeared to be bronze. Could it possibly fit the tower gate? I ran back and felt for the lock and tried the key. The

SHE TURNED HER HEAD TOWARDS ME...AND THERE WAS NOUGHT BUT BLACKNESS WHERE HER FACE SHOULD HAVE BEEN.

portal opened on creaking hinges. As I crossed the threshold I thought, why would a dead man's buried key open a locked tower?

I strained to see into the darkness ahead, the air was dank and cool and smelled of moss. I pulled out my tinder box and made light. In the flickering shadows, I caught sight of a rat darting away, and saw a ruined staircase to an upper floor lying in a heap of stone. The walls and ceiling were blackened and cracked in places, and aside from fragments and splinters of wood there was nothing else to be seen. I was fatigued, and removing only my hat, I lay down to rest. The light died. I heard a faint fluttering and chittering of bats high above me. Shuddering at the memory of the creature which had attacked me outside, I wrapped my cloak around my face and neck in the darkness.

...In a dream I climbed the tower. Golden sunlight poured in through the windows as I passed. The walls and stairs were intact. At the top there was a room with a single carved wooden chair at its centre, with a window on either side. A long haired woman in antique dress was standing across the chamber with her back to me, talking to something she held before her and caressed. Opening her hands, a small creature flapped up into the shadowed recesses of the high rafters. She turned her head towards me... nothing but blackness where her face should have been. Then I was falling; the tower dissolved, and I fell down, down into the cold earth, the sound of my heart beating so loudly as to deafen me...

I woke from the nightmare with my heart racing and a feeling of dread such as I had never felt before. It was a fear of the outside, of the withered garden, of what might be clawing at the stones of my refuge. As I shook my head to clear the cobwebs of sleep away, I thought I heard a faint, deep, distant heartbeat that filled my veins with ice. With shaking hands I found and donned my hat, then slowly, as if against my will, I rose on stiff legs and walked to the tower door, opened it and stepped out into the silvery blue moonlight and cold, silent air. I felt for my sword hilt. Some of my pride returned, and with it a measure of my natural courage. That a nobleman of France should feel such fear, and having fought and won two duels in his life at that!

There came a soft sound, a sort of rattling, clacking noise. It seemed to come from the twisted boles of the apple trees near the point at which I had entered this place. There was a palpable sense of evil. I felt desolation and weariness emanating from the ruined orchard. I stumbled forward on leaden feet, shaking with the horror of what I knew I must find. I peered through the moonlight at the animal bones at the foot of one of the misted, stunted growths.

But they were not animal bones.

As I watched, rooted to the spot, the bones articulated themselves and writhed upwards into a mocking parody of a man's form. And the thing held a rusted knife with which it tried to prune and cut the tree, pawing at the branches with an obscene intimacy. As I looked on aghast, I saw a single, swollen, blood red apple hanging from a gnarled branch where none had been the night before, in the weird blue-grey radiance, the skull face turned to look at me. I fled in panic, through the decaying outer wall.

I remember little of that mad flight; a glimmer of light was just beginning to come into the eastern sky as I found the western edge of that dreadful moorland. After many miles I had to rest once more, and I found welcome solace in a berry patch skirting a lowland wood. The rays of the sun did little to warm the chill in my heart as I fell into a troubled sleep.

By the afternoon I walked on, sore from the long journey downslope. My mind whirled with memories of the terrifying night, and I couldn't help but try to make sense of what had happened. In time I came to a narrow path through an open woodland, which met a road and then wound on some half a mile to an ancient tavern, where I gratefully satisfied my hunger with bread, cheese and wine. Remembering to maintain my disguise, I fell into conversation with the elderly innkeeper at a booth in the low beamed, smoky tap room. In time I asked him about the tower in the hills.

"Well, young master," he said, hunching his thin shoulders and knitting his low brows. "Nobody from these parts will travel that lonely way, and it is said to be an unlucky place in any account. But, mind you..." and he wiped his hands on his apron and leant his bald head in a little closer, "There is a tale about that place that few know of nowadays. I heard it from my grandfather as a boy, and he said it was told to him by an old man who claimed to have seen the demise of the estate. It was said that early in the last century, an old Lord had had a hold in yonder hills. Now he was cruel to his hounds, his servants and men, the bats in his belfry and even his wife, who was said to be fair beautiful; and all he loved were his vineyard and orchard and his crops that kept him fat and drunk. Anyway, he beat and neglected his wife, if you take my meaning, Sir, and she being far younger than he, took a younger man for a lover. Now the Lord found out about this, and in a mad rage he murdered the young man and locked the poor girl in his own keep and burned it. Such an evil deed. The poor creature. And 'tis also said that as the flames licked higher, she cursed him to find no peace or rest, but to tend his garden forever. And he laughed. Then he spread wild tales about her being in league with the Devil. He was powerful and had many friends, and was beyond the power of justice." I paled upon hearing this, and asked him how this man had met his end. "Ah, well it is told that his servants left him one by one, until only one loyal old man remained to his service. Fleeing to a nearby village, he consumed far too much wine and related a wild tale about his master locking himself in his blackened tower. Then he had seen lights at the uppermost window, along with a hideous shrieking sound; then the old lord falling, screaming from a window. The terrified servant could think of nothing else but to inter the corpse without last rites and then he ran, fearing that he would be blamed for the old man's death." And with that he wandered away to leave me brooding into my wine cup.

So, there is my tale. And in more ways than one, this new world to which my family and I fled holds less terrors for me than the old one.

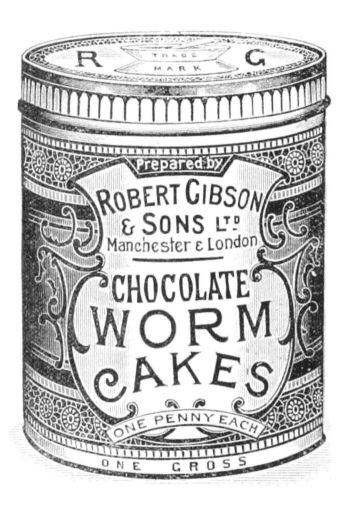

CONTRIBUTORS

MATT HOPKINS is a Welsh writer, guitar teacher and international assassin. He also hopes to become a full time liar. He enjoys short walks in the park and using light switches. He has so far been short-listed for nothing, but hopes that this will soon prove to be less true than it currently is. Hate mail can be sent here: *witchfindermusic@gmail.com*

CHERYL LOUISE LLOYD is a mature student on an Access course, with a view to an English and Creative Writing degree afterwards. She writes because she can't not do it. She loves M.R James, old grave-yards, Victorian Post-Mortem photographs and stories where the everyday becomes chilling and disturbing. She has had some poetry published in magazines and an anthology, this is her first story submission.

ALYSSA COOPER is a professionally trained artist and graphic designer, combining a traditional foundation with modern flair. She began studying art in 2008, attending York University in Toronto for two years, where she studied visual arts, with a major in painting and drawing. In 2010, she transferred to the advanced Graphic Design program at Durham College, where she received multiple awards for her illustrative abilities. She is currently living in Kingston, Ontario, where she is self employed as a freelance designer and illustrator. Her print designs have been used prominently by a number of local and international companies, and her illustrations can be seen in prominent publications, such as *Postscripts to Darkness*, an Ottawa-based anthology, and *Ontario Garlic*, a title by History Press. Find her:
alyssacooperarts.com
facebook.com/AlyssaCooperArts

MELANIE MARSHALL is a freelance editor living in Somerset with her husband, toddler son, baby daughter and two cats. Back in 2004 she completed the prestigious MA in Creative Writing at the University of East Anglia. She has had her short stories published by *Pen & Inc Press*, *The Moth*, *Momaya Press* and *Prole Books*. Her unpublished novel, *Noir Gris*, was longlisted for Mslexia's 2013 Novel Competition. She enjoys good coffee, real ale and dark tales by Angela Carter, Robert Aickman, M.R. James and Jeremy Dyson.

CHRIS LAMBERT has been writing for an age. He has worked variously as a playwright, a teacher, a writer of short stories and a liar. He is the writer of "Tales from the Black Meadow" a collection of short stories concerning a mysterious place on the North York Moors. Starburst Magazine describes his work as a "paranoia-inducing sucker punch". He is currently working on two new collections of short stories that should be released late next year. His plays include: *Loving Chopin*, *Edmund Son of Gloucester*, *Ship of Fools*, and *The Simple Process of Alchemy*. He has had short stories published by Seance at Syd's, The Dead Files and Tales of the Damned. *lambertthewriter.blogspot.co.uk* *blackmeadowtales.blogspot.co.uk*

LEONA PRESTON lives in the East Midlands and spends her waking hours working feverishly as a graphic designer. By night and in the company of moonlight and taxidermy wildings, she loves nothing better than to illustrate unconventional characters and the peculiar worlds they inhabit. A lifelong fan of classic literature and a good ghost story, she occasionally endeavours to write and is currently working on a graphic adaptation of the 1846 penny dreadful *Sweeney Todd*. 'Master of Escape' Harry Houdini and his link to the shadowy world of Spiritualism is just one of her quirky interests.

MARIA J PÉREZ CUERVO was born in Spain, but has lived in England for eleven years. It was here that she completed her MA in Archaeology for Screen Media, winning the Mick Aston prize for her dissertation on archaeology and the occult in popular culture. She's worked in television, e-media and printed media, and writes regularly about myth, history and

mystery for *Fortean Times*. "The Village Below" is her first attempt at publishing fiction. You can reach her at *www.mjpcuervo.com*

STUART SNELSON'S stories have appeared in *3:AM*, *Ambit*, *Bare Fiction*, *The Bohemyth*, *HOAX*, *Lighthouse*, *Popshot* and *Structo*, among others. He has been twice nominated for the Pushcart Prize. Links to previous stories can be found at *stuartsnelson.wordpress.com*. He lives in London where he is currently working on his second novel. He can be found on Twitter @stuartsnelson

LYNN HARDAKER is a Canadian artist and writer currently living in Germany. Her work has appeared, or is forthcoming in *Mythic Delirium*, *Scheherezade's Bequest*, *Goblin Fruit*, and *Ideomancer*.

REBECCA PARFITT has worked in publishing for over eight years. She has also been widely published in magazines and anthologies. She co-edited a collection of new Gothic fiction: *A Flock of Shadows*, (Parthian, 2014). In her spare time she can be found performing with ropes and silks at the circus or exorcising her pet rats, Otto and Houdini.

NATHANIEL and CATHERINE WINTER-HÉBERT are the creative minds at Winter-Hébert design studio. They work remotely from their home in the wilds of rural Quebec, where Nathaniel immerses himself in typefaces and Catherine obsesses over grids. Together, they craft works of design brilliance from their forest abode whilst their hand-raised sparrows sit upon their shoulders, offering art direction advice. *winterhebert.com*

Lightning Source UK Ltd.
Milton Keynes UK
UKOW07f2124161215

264829UK00006B/100/P